This book belongs

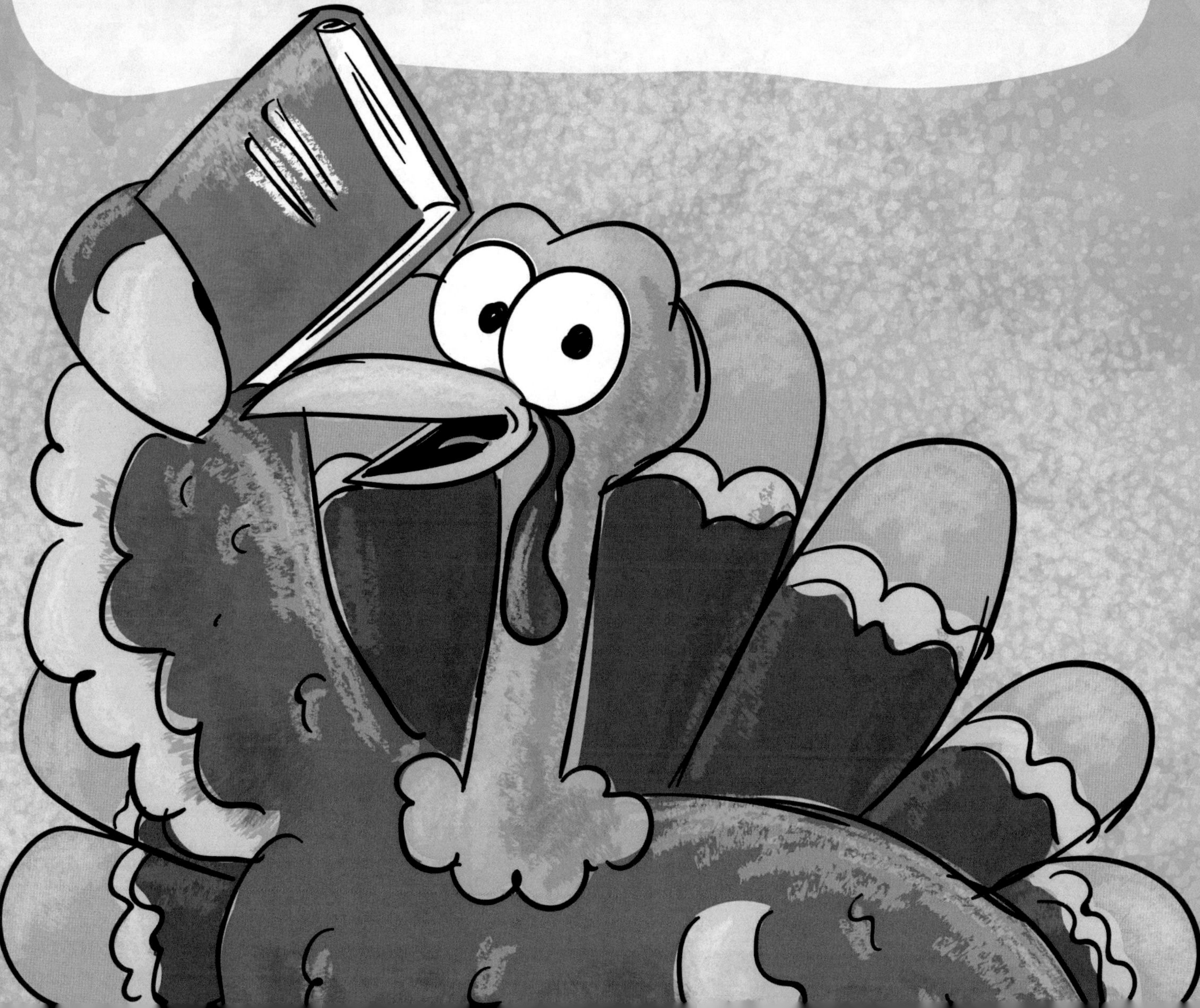

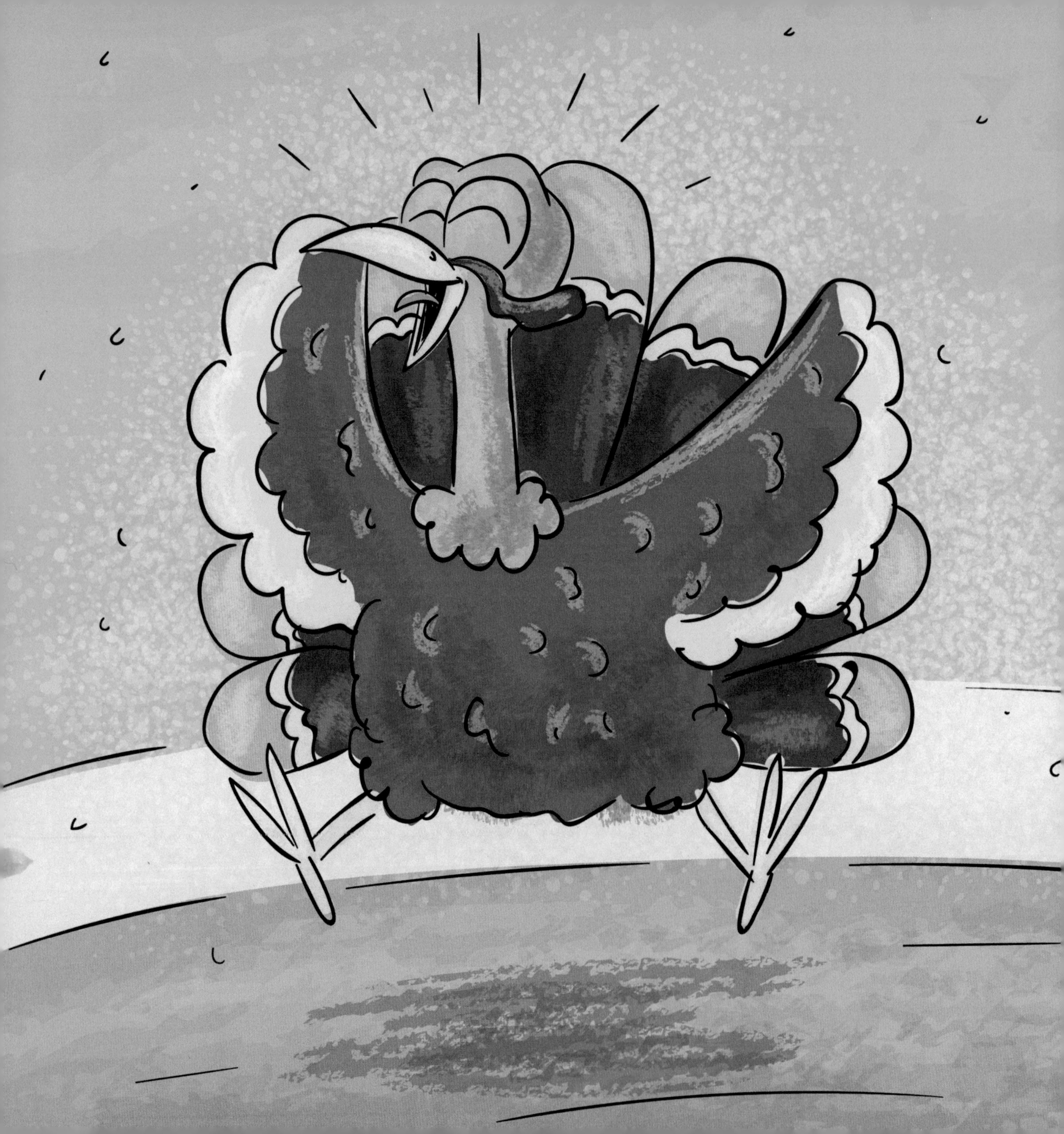

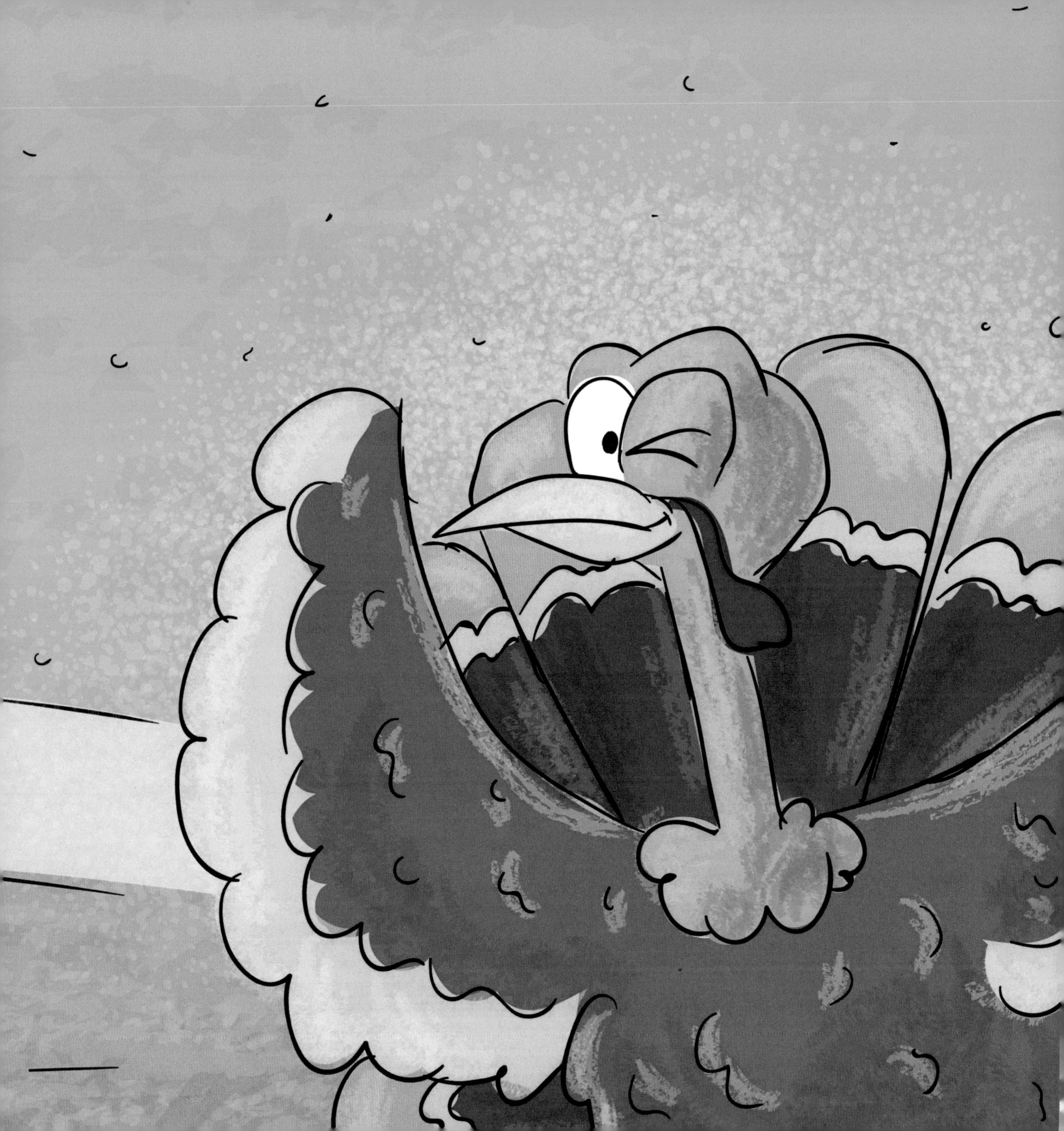

Printed and bound in the USA. 978-1-63731-283-4

Visit us at NeverEverBooks.com

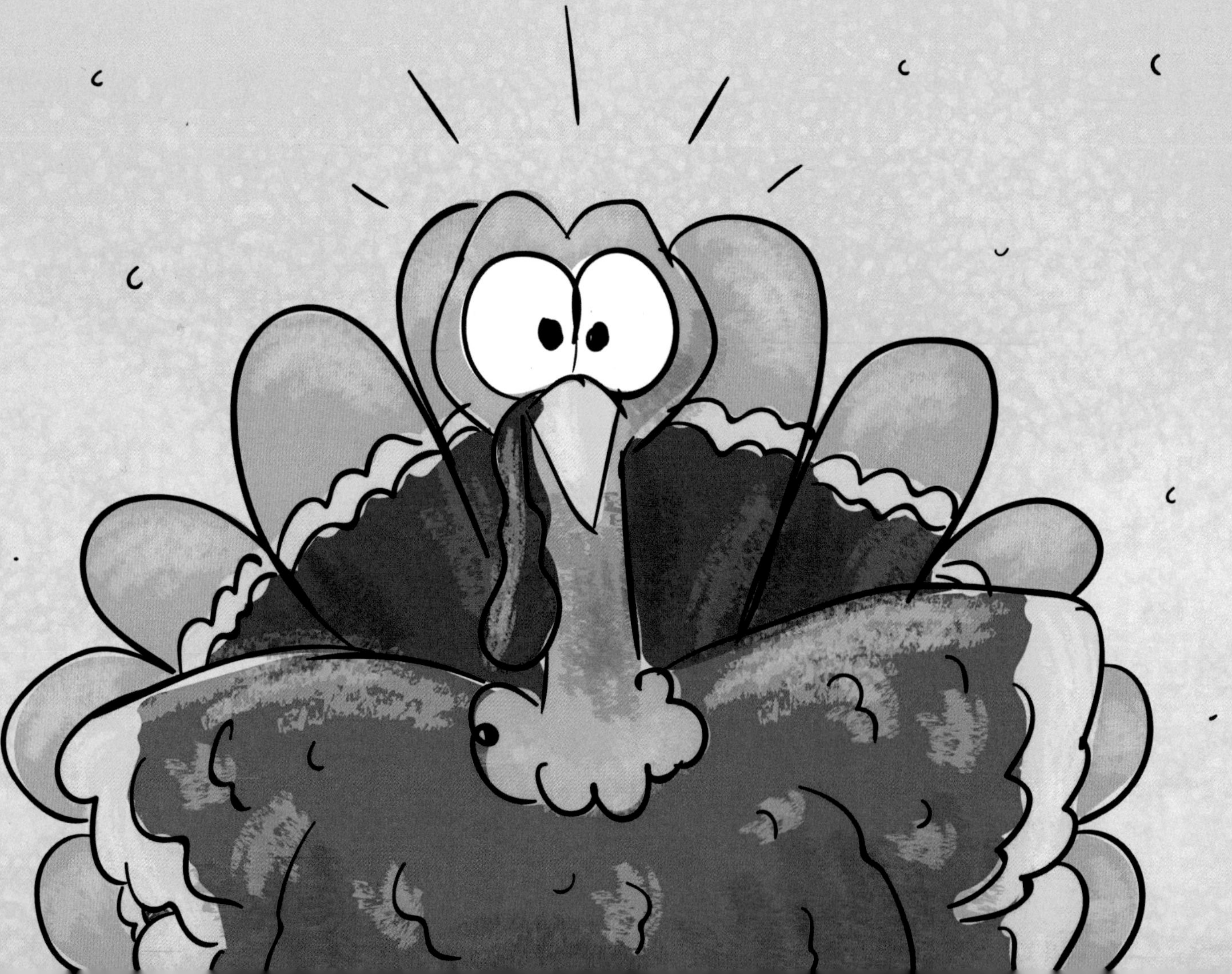

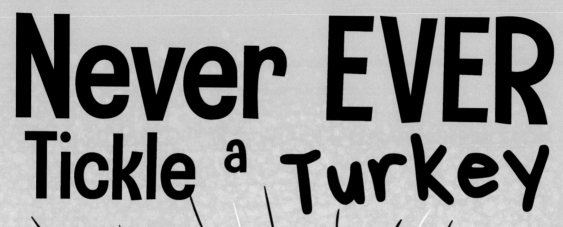

Never EVER Tickle a Turkey

By Adam Wallace
and Mary Nhin

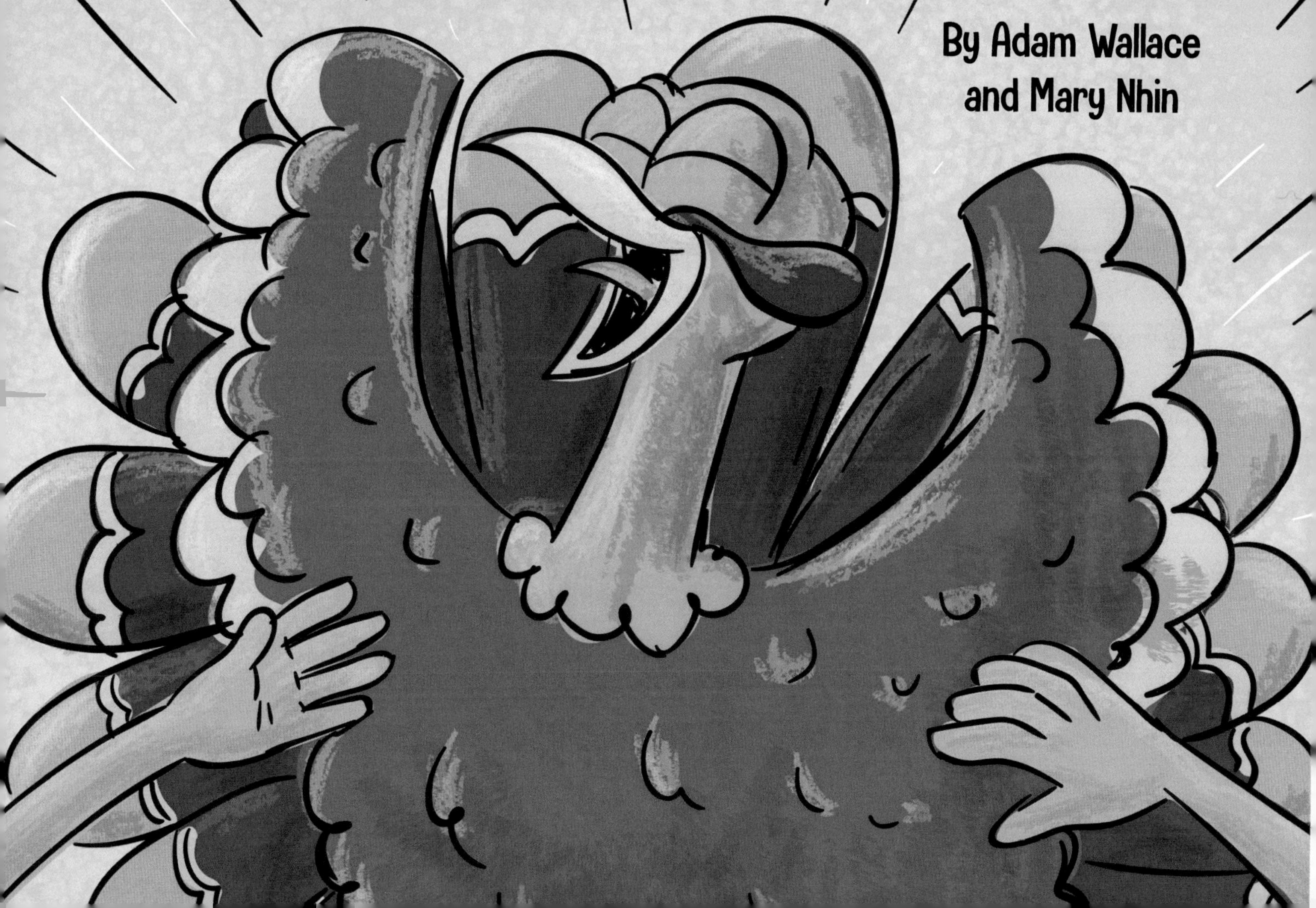

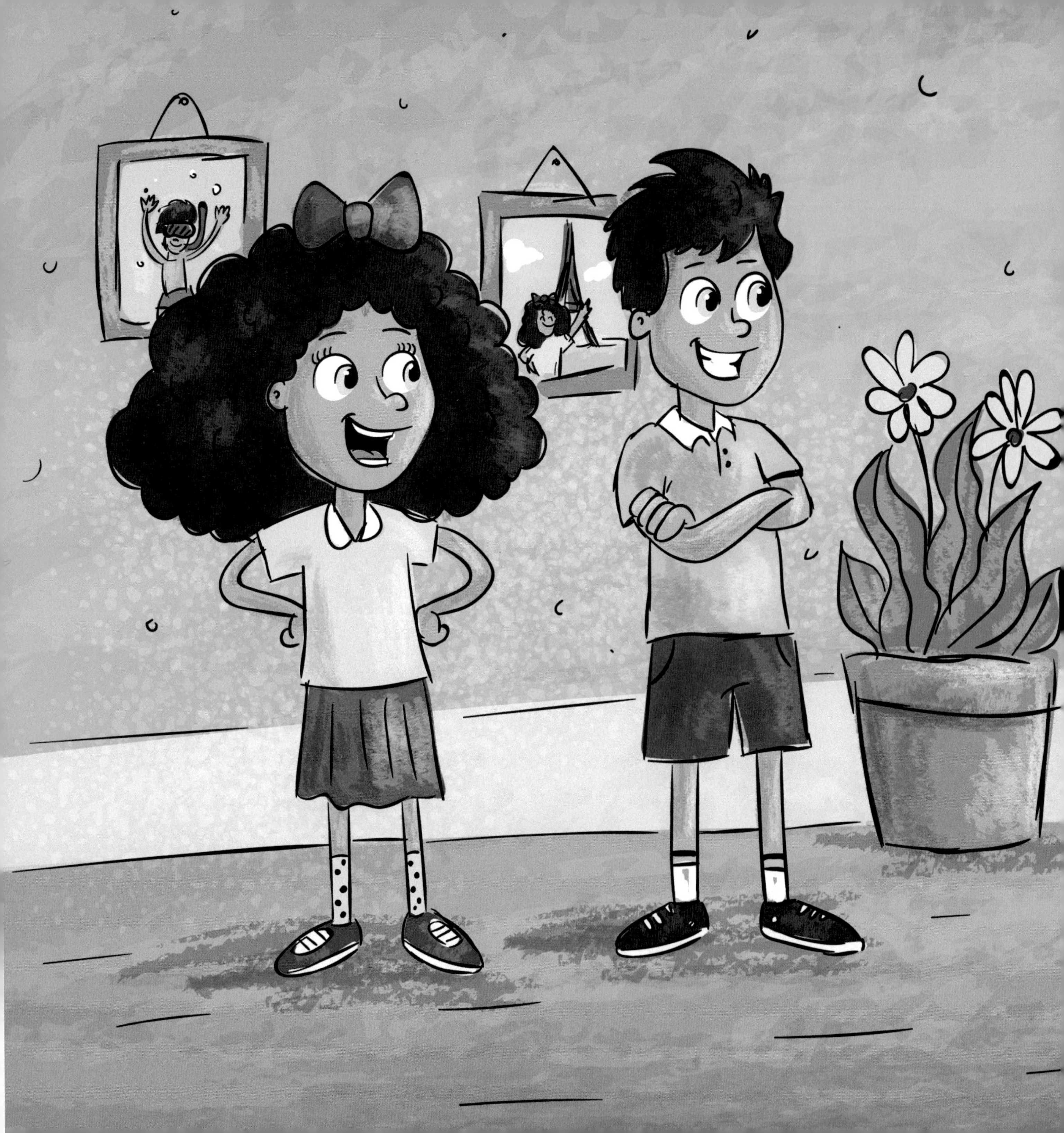

There are things that you are going to do,
That will not go astray.
But some experiences **WILL** go bad,
In **EVERY** single way!

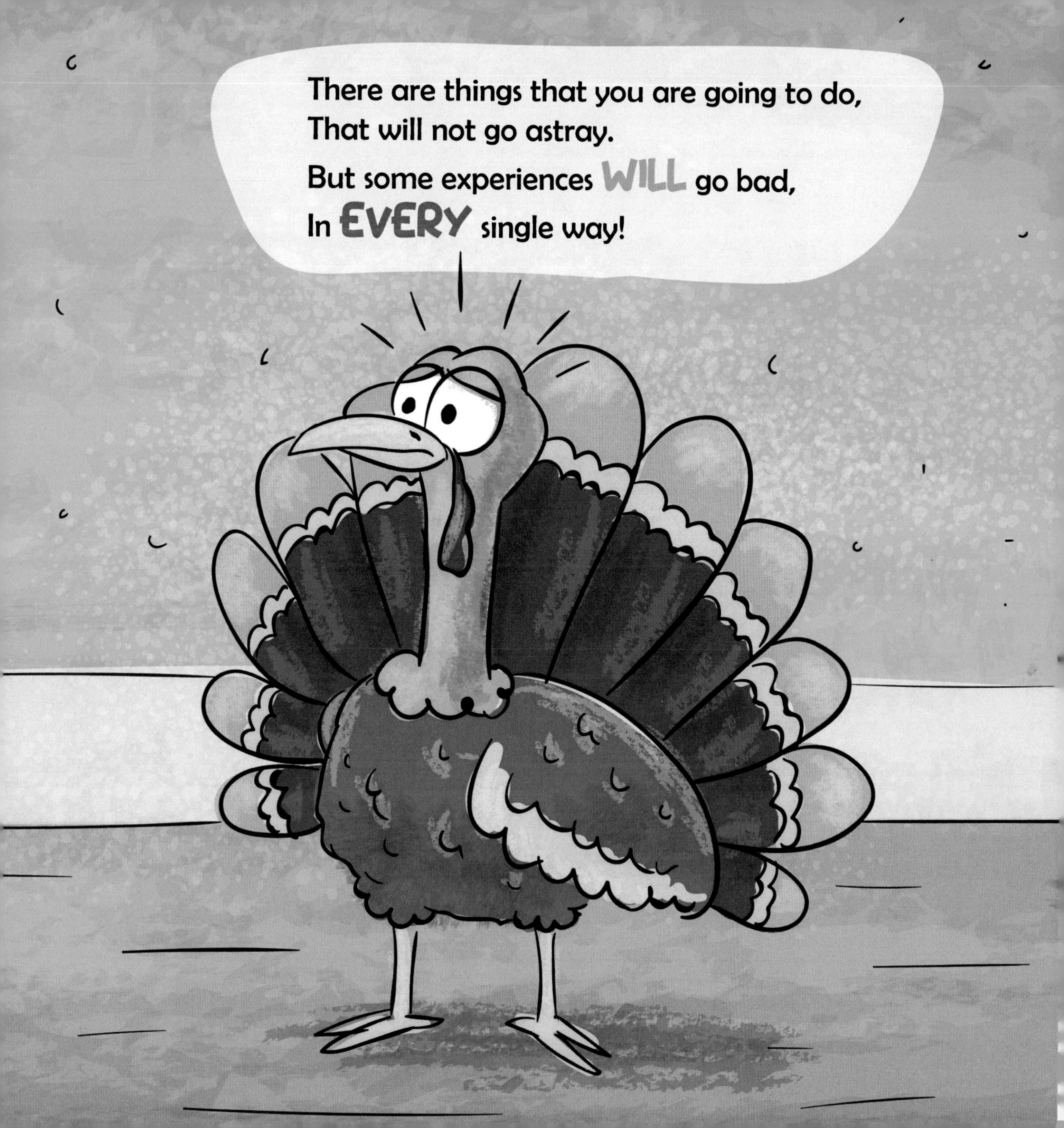

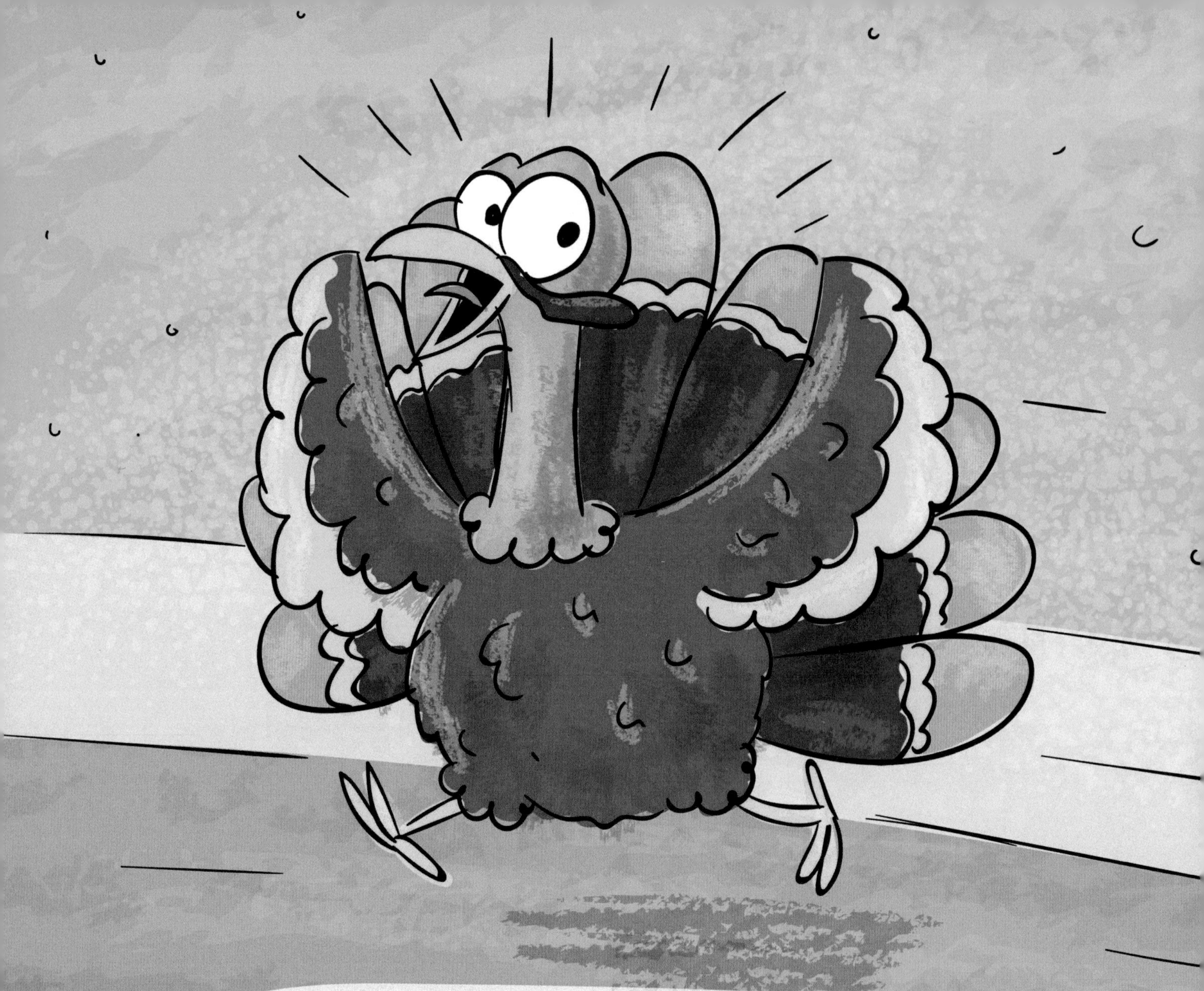

Never **EVER** tickle a turkey,
Not that I think you would.
But stranger things have happened,
Which I've never understood.

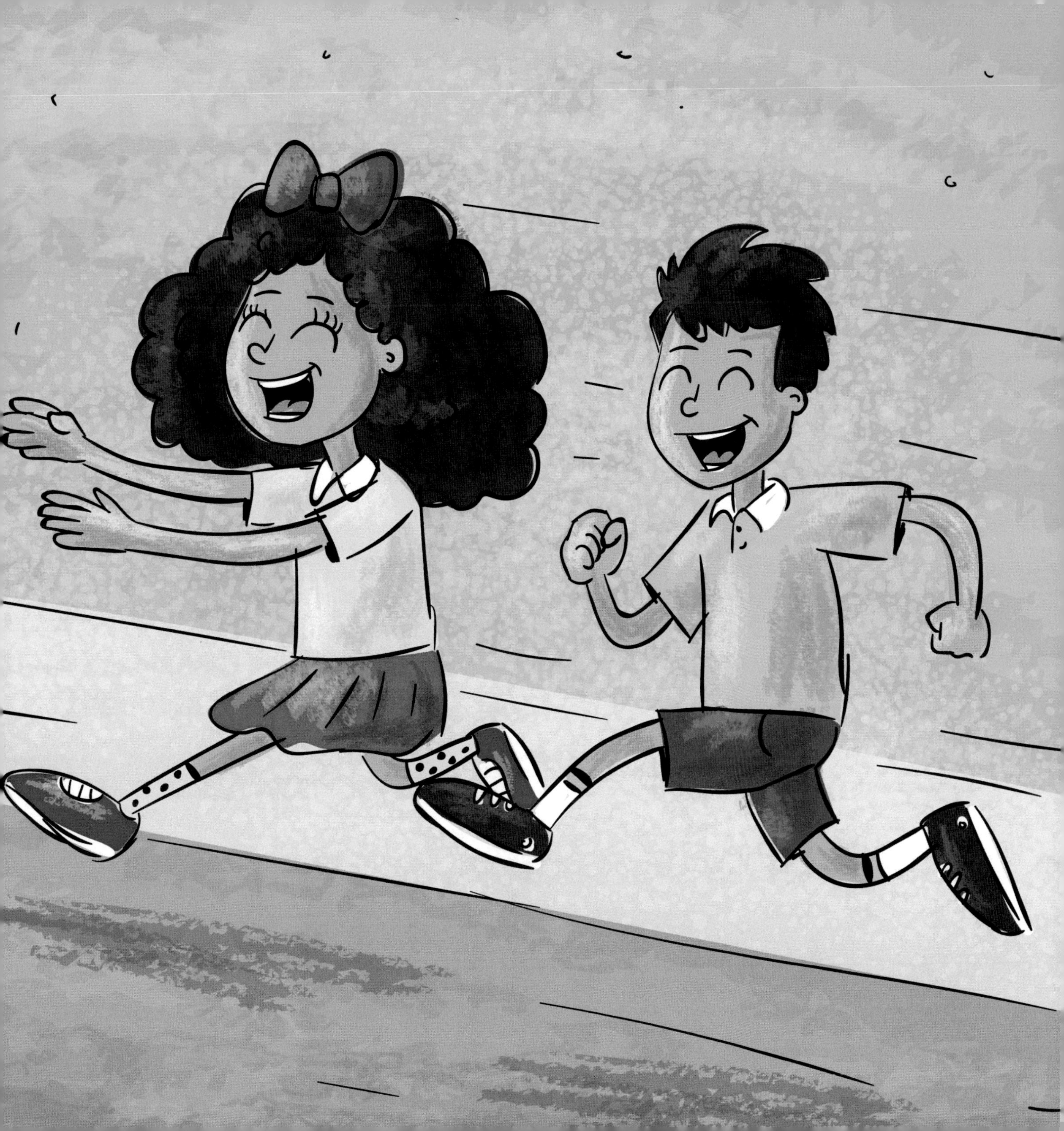

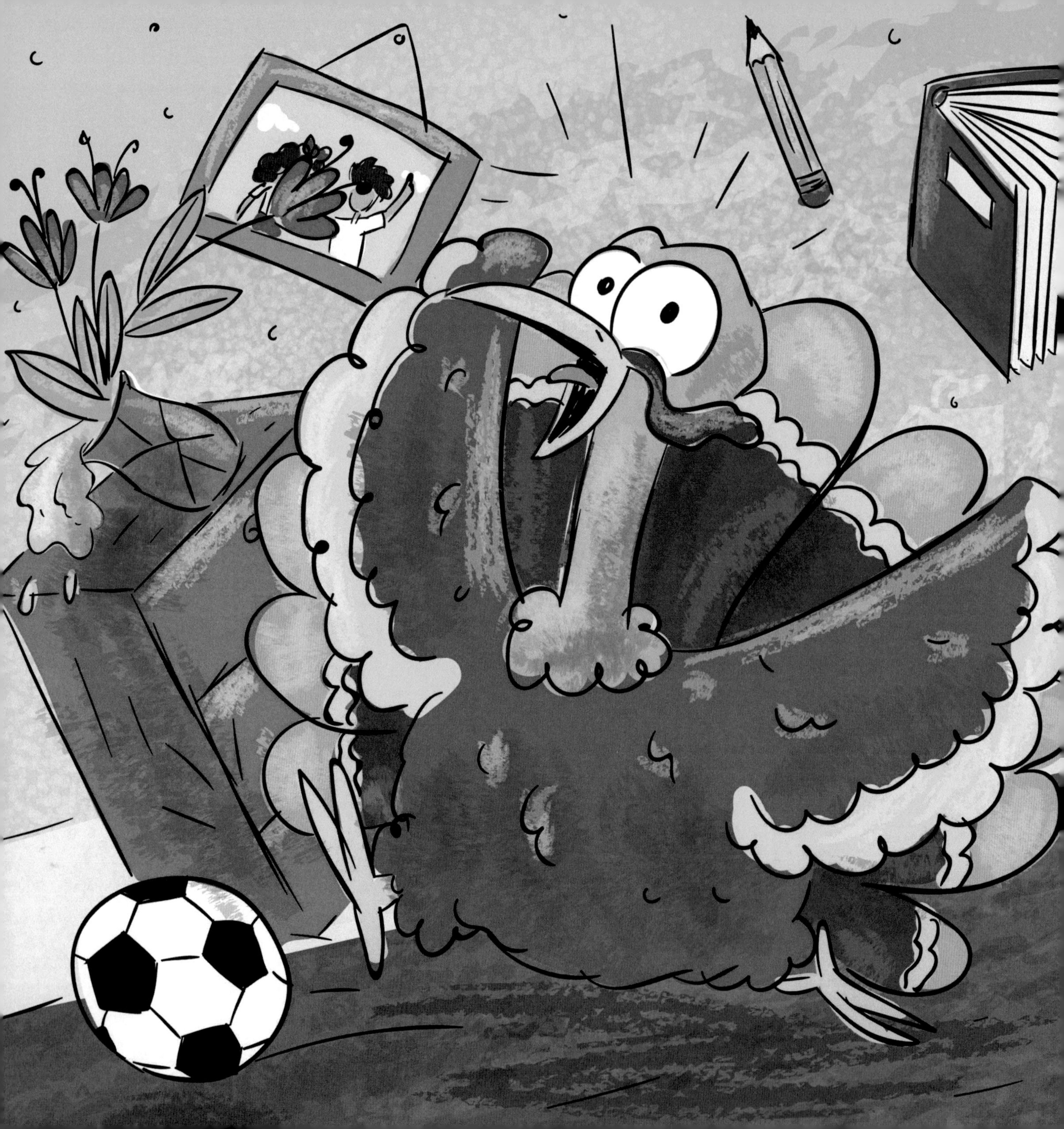

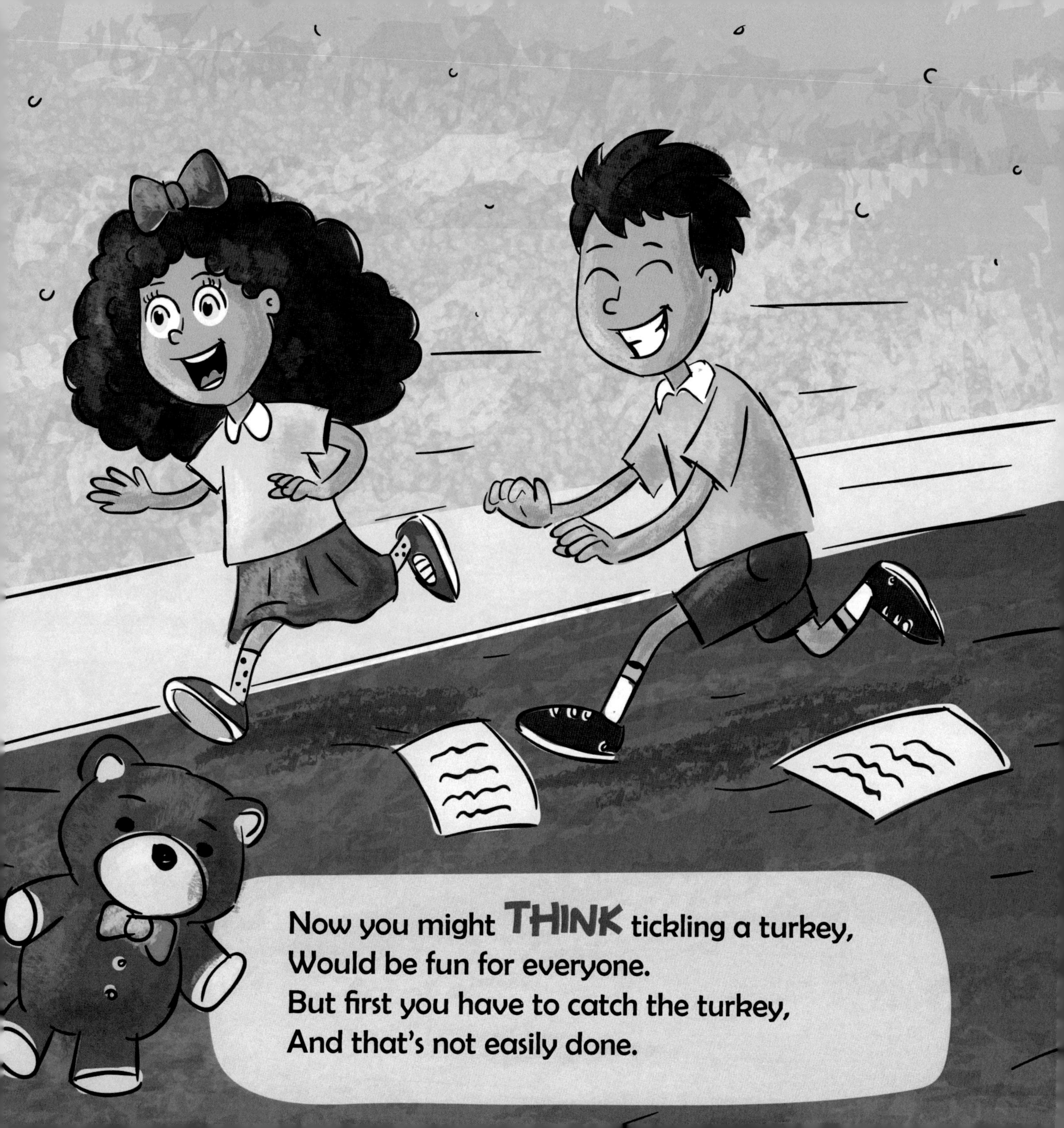

Now you might **THINK** tickling a turkey,
Would be fun for everyone.
But first you have to catch the turkey,
And that's not easily done.

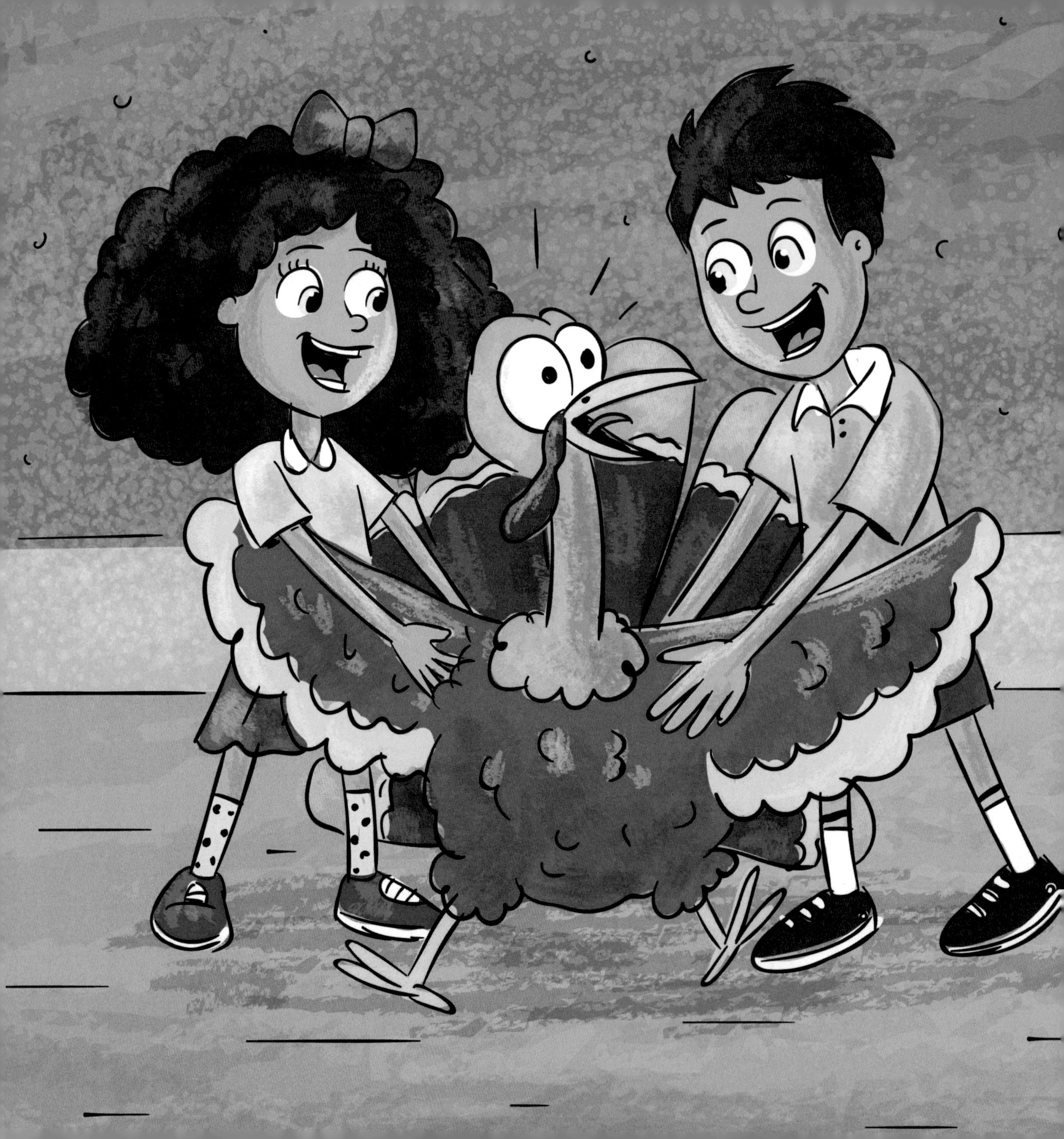

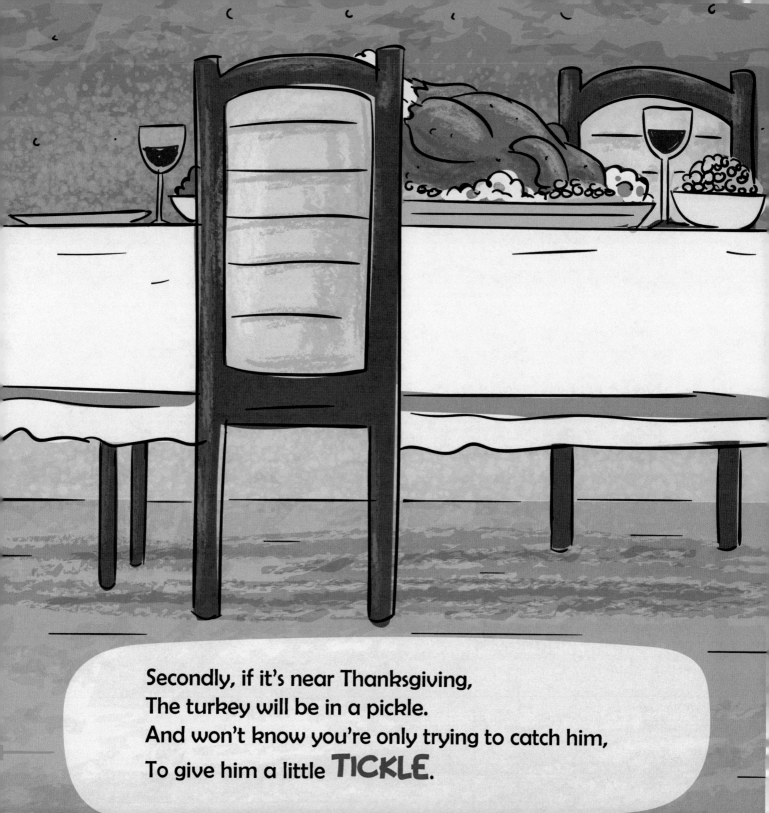

Secondly, if it's near Thanksgiving,
The turkey will be in a pickle.
And won't know you're only trying to catch him,
To give him a little **TICKLE**.

And finally, the most serious reason,
And a STINKY one to boot.
Is tickling makes turkeys laugh so much,
The turkey's gonna toot!

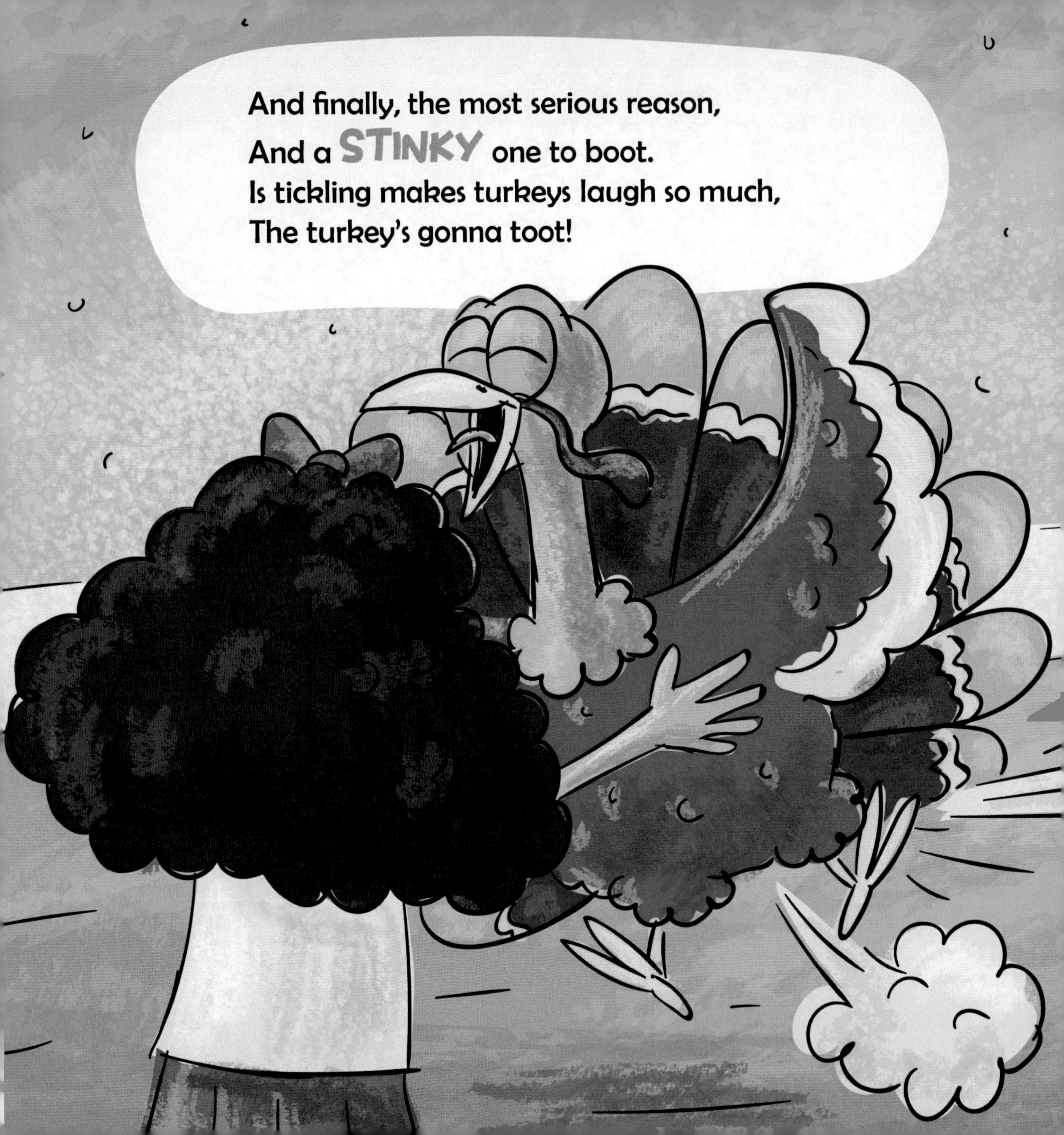

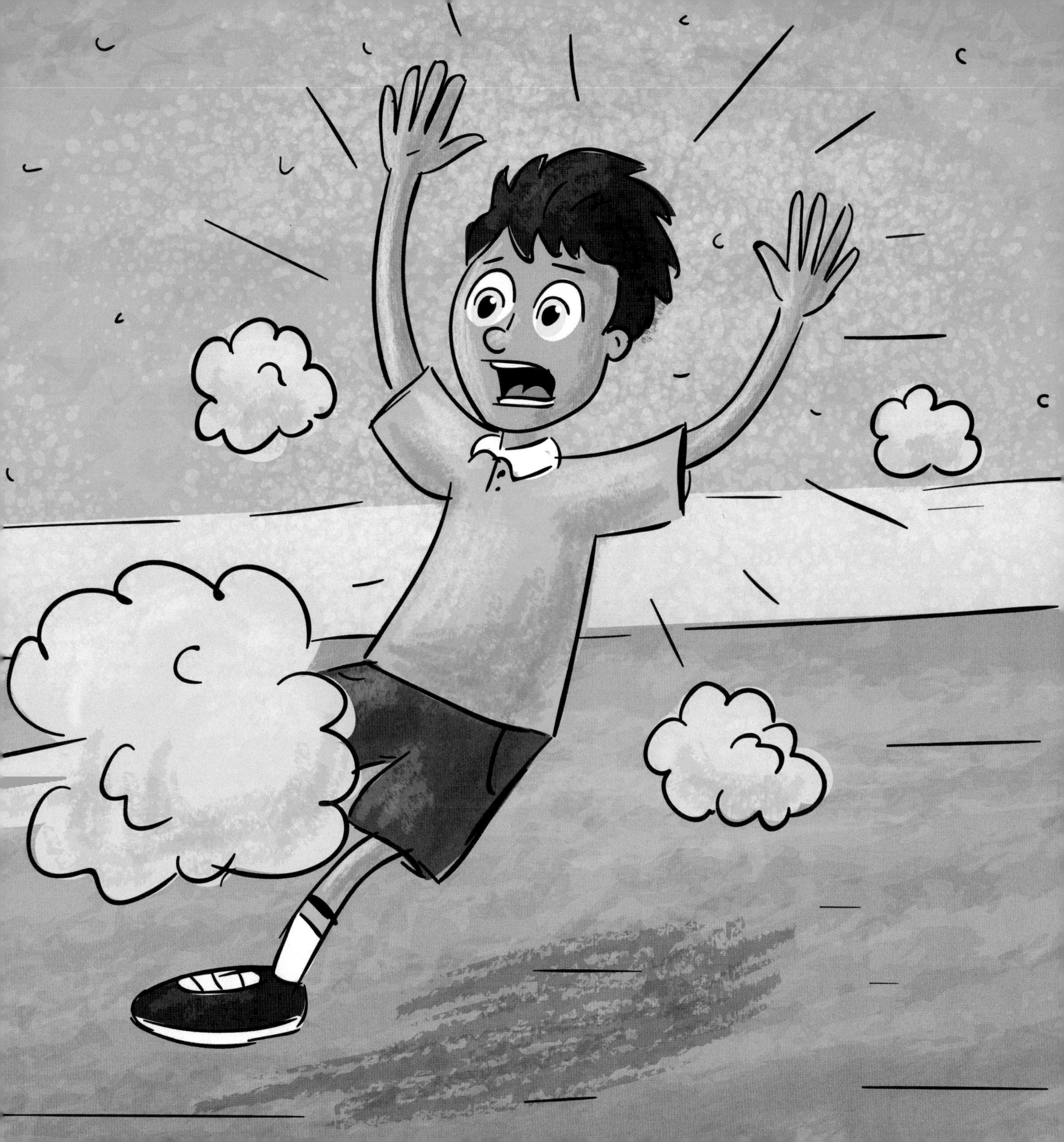

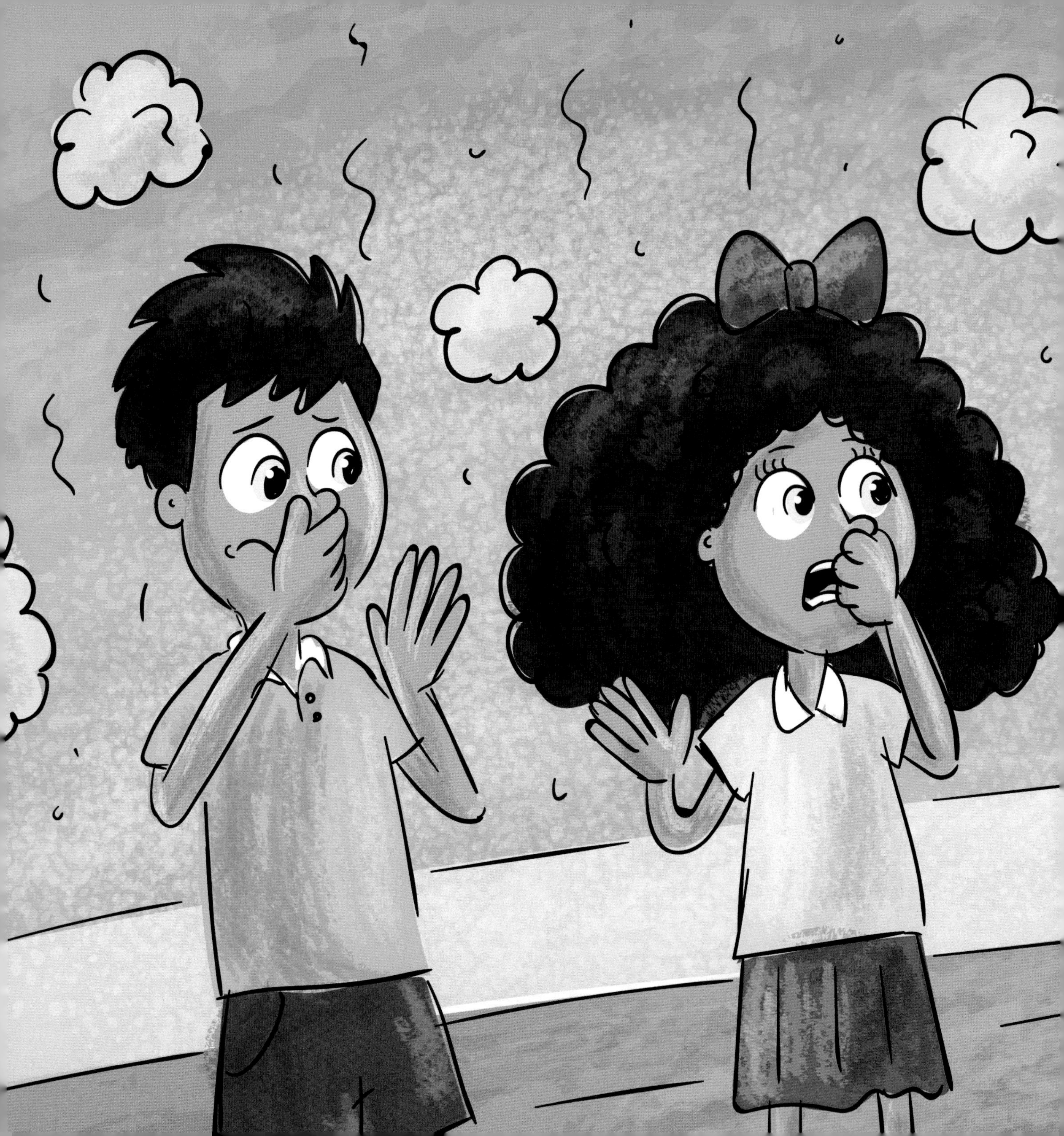

Also, never **EVER** trust a turkey,
And if you think you should.
There's a chance the turkey will trick you,
And that would not be good!

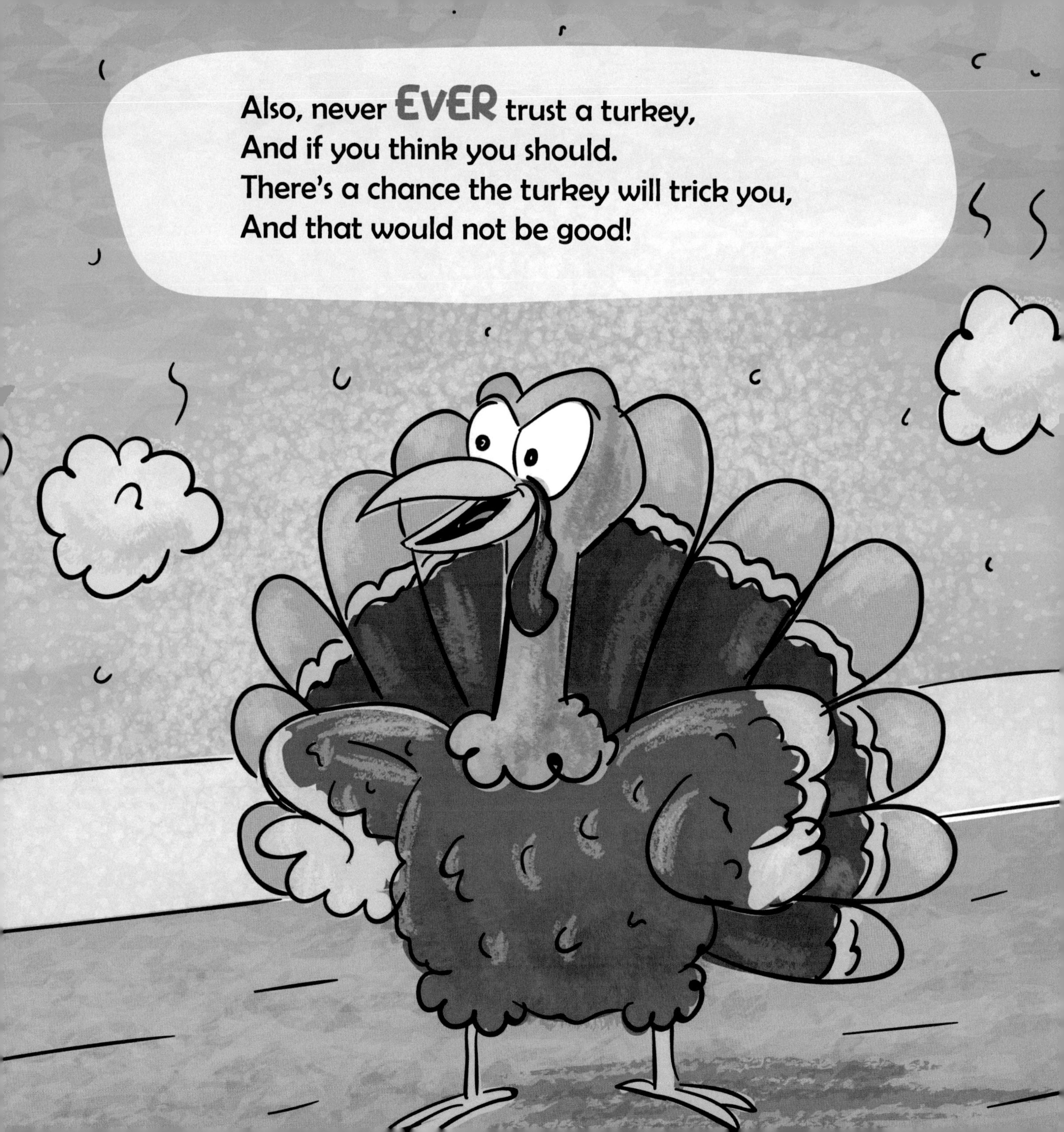

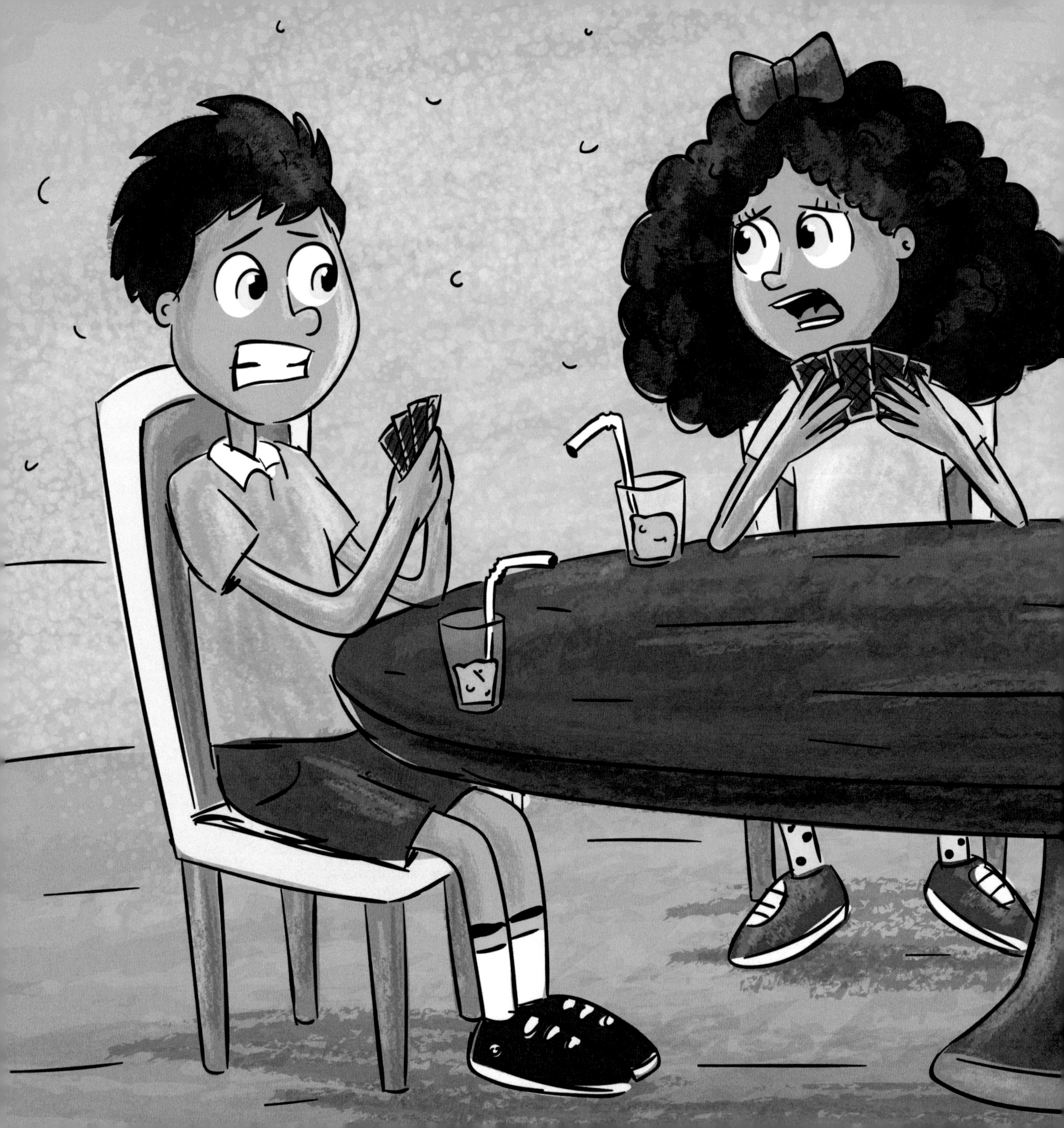

They'll hide cards under their feathers,
So that they'll **ALWAYS** win.
And if they lose, they'll take the cards,
And throw them in the bin!

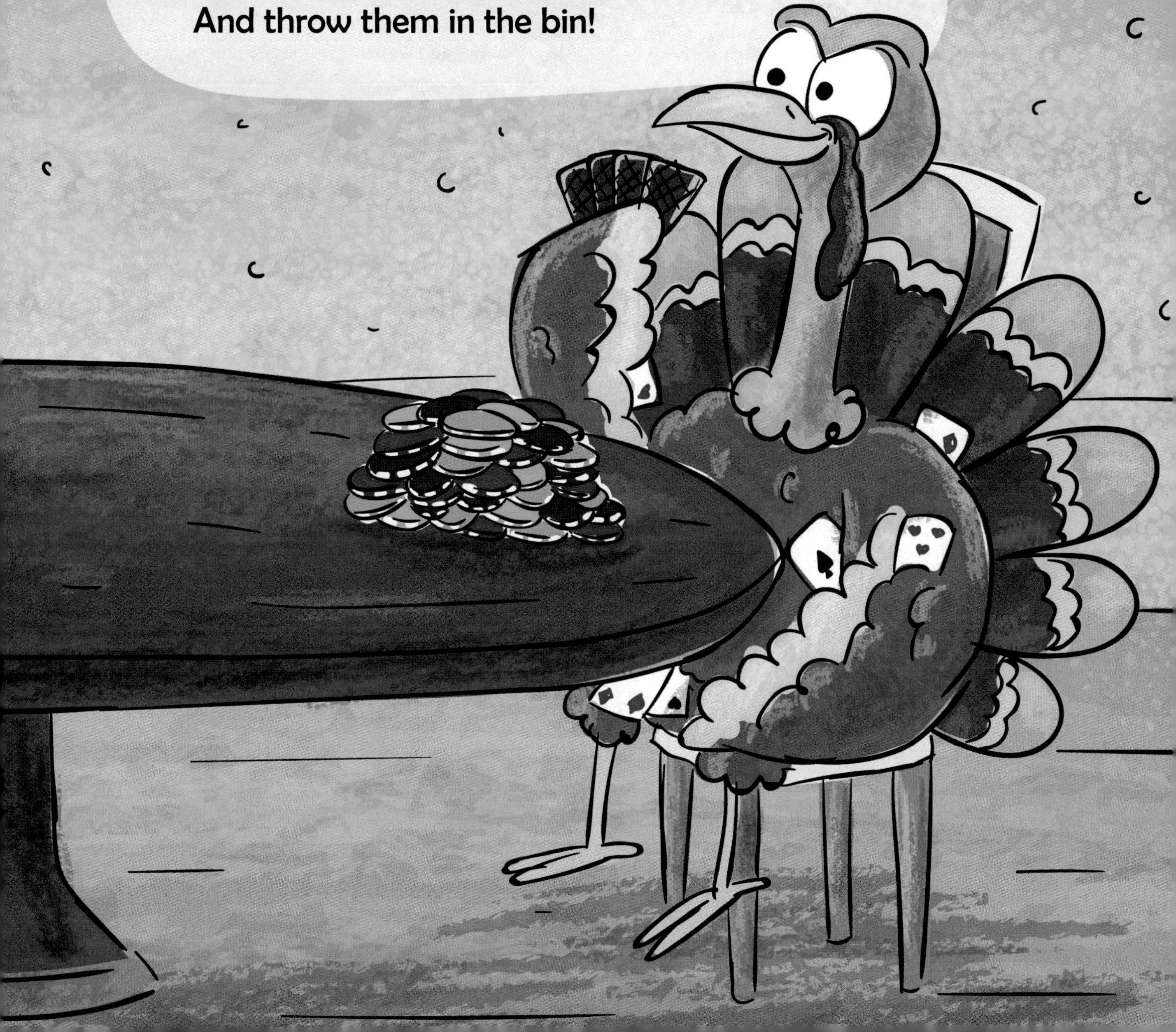

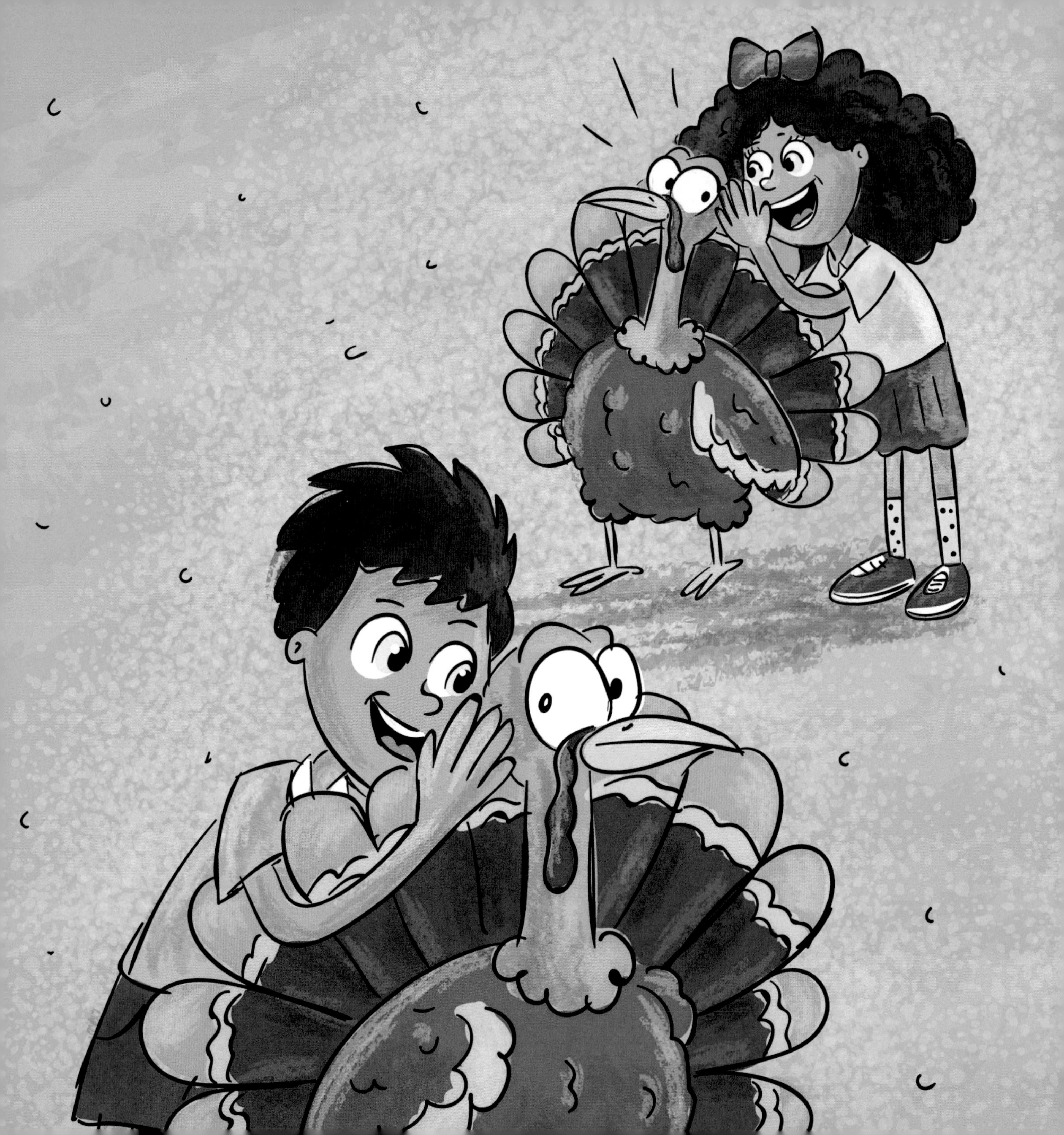

And don't tell a turkey a secret,
THAT should never be done,
NEVER EVER trust a turkey, I said,
They tell secrets to **EVERYONE**!

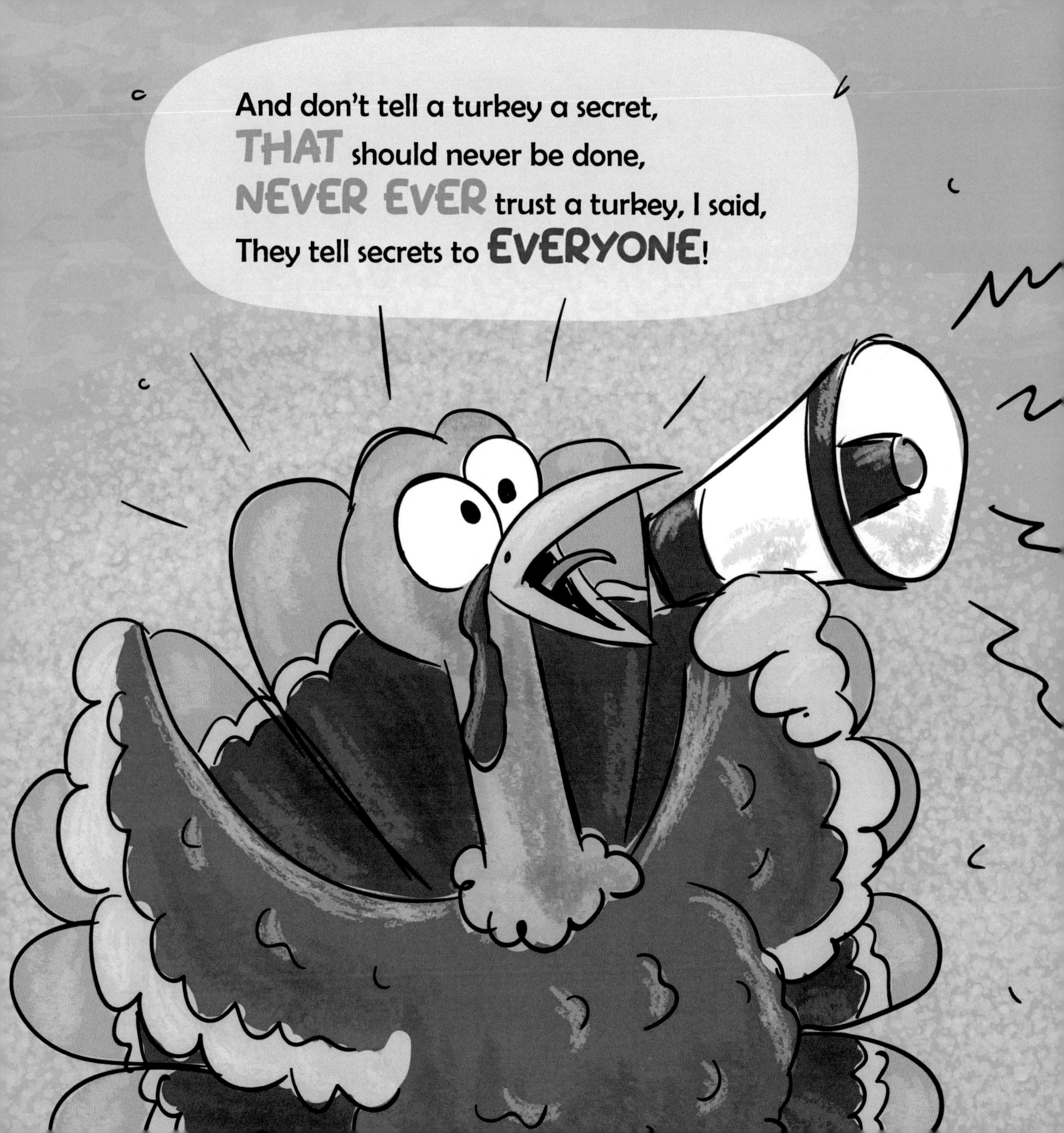

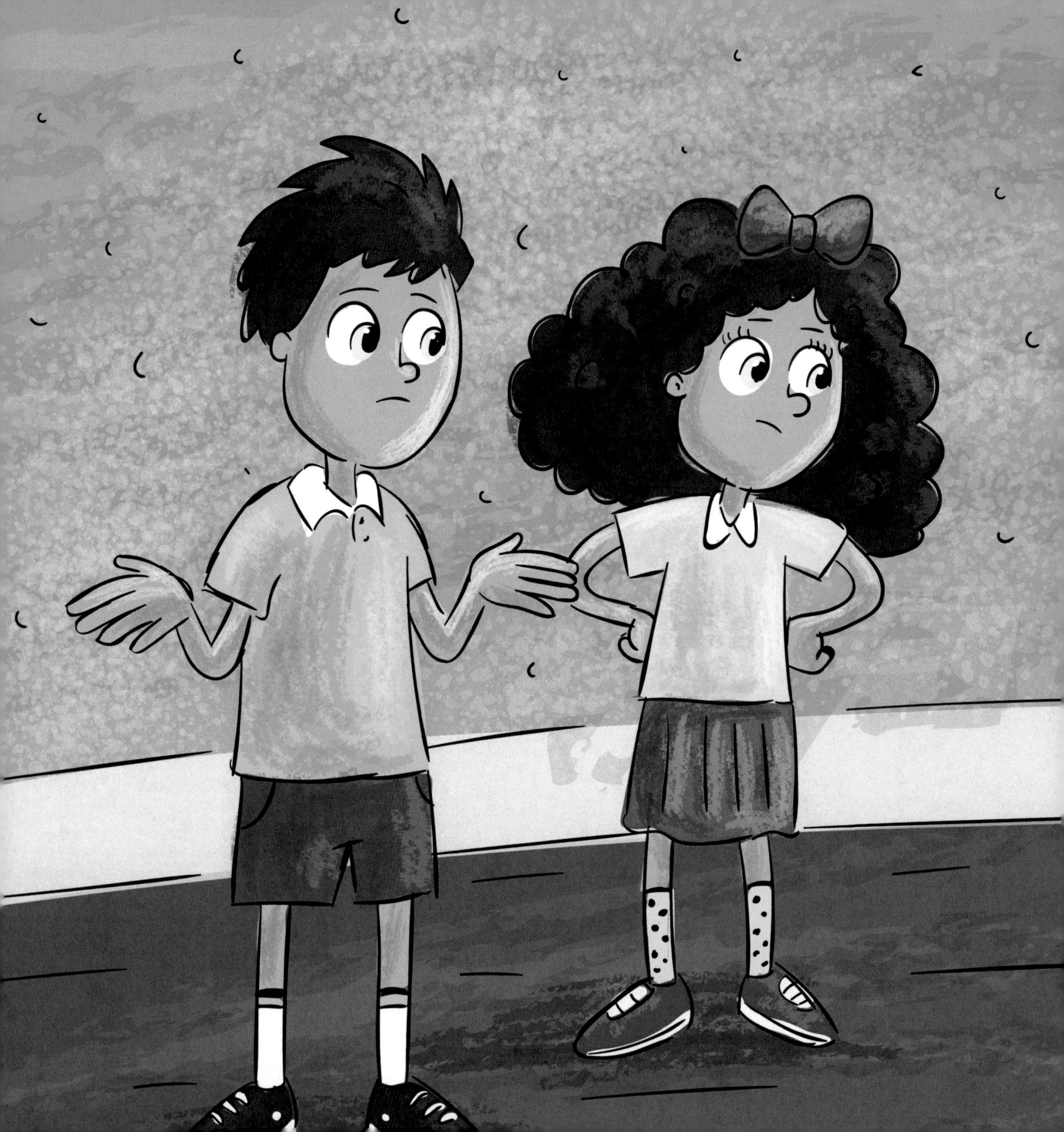

And, finally, never **EVER** translate a turkey,
I wouldn't if I could.
All you'll hear is turkeys complaining,
NOTHING they say is good!

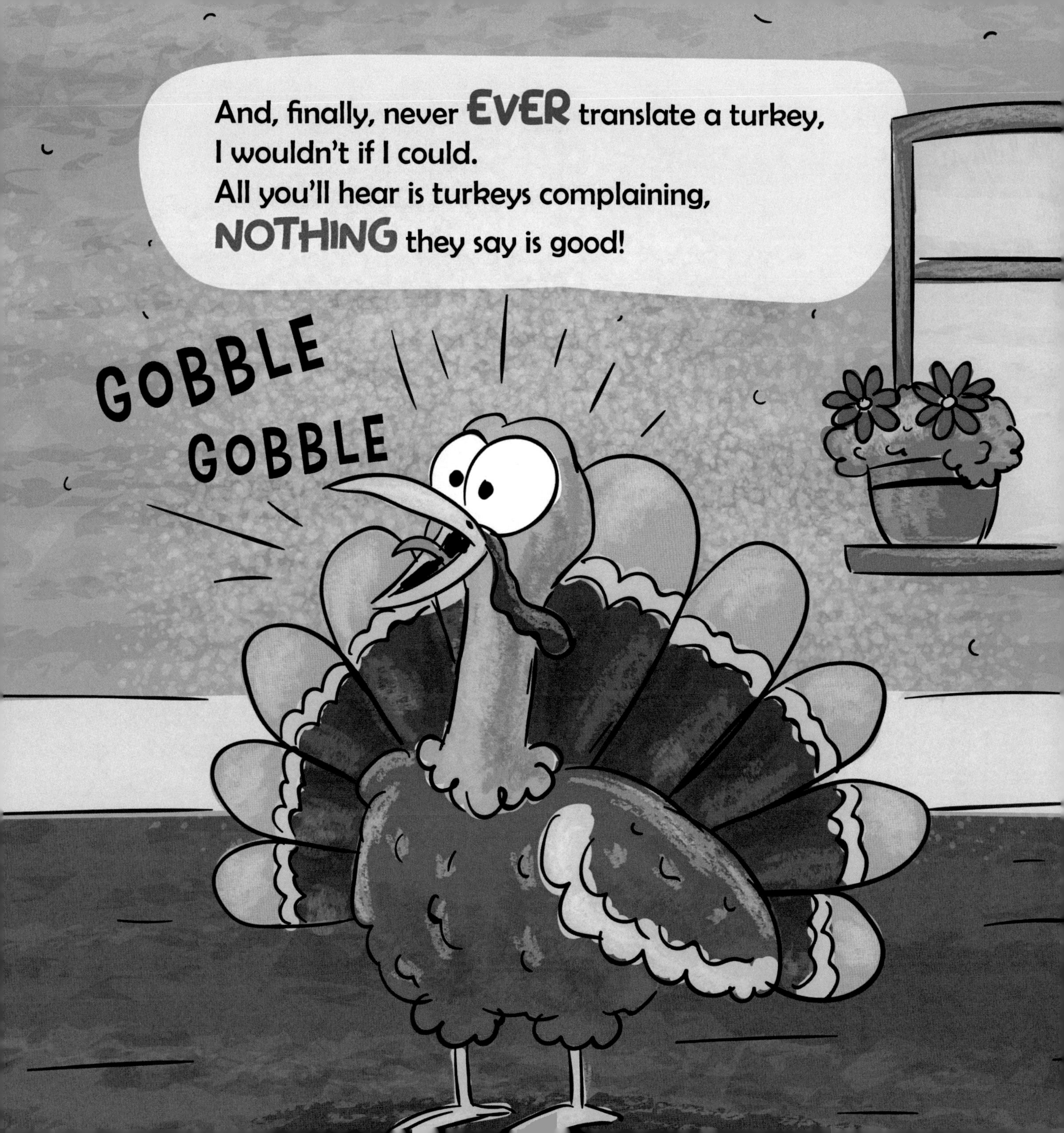
GOBBLE
GOBBLE
GOBBLE

They all hate waddling around on the ground,
Turkeys long to fly.
So ALLLLLL day long they'll complain about that,
It will make you want to cry.

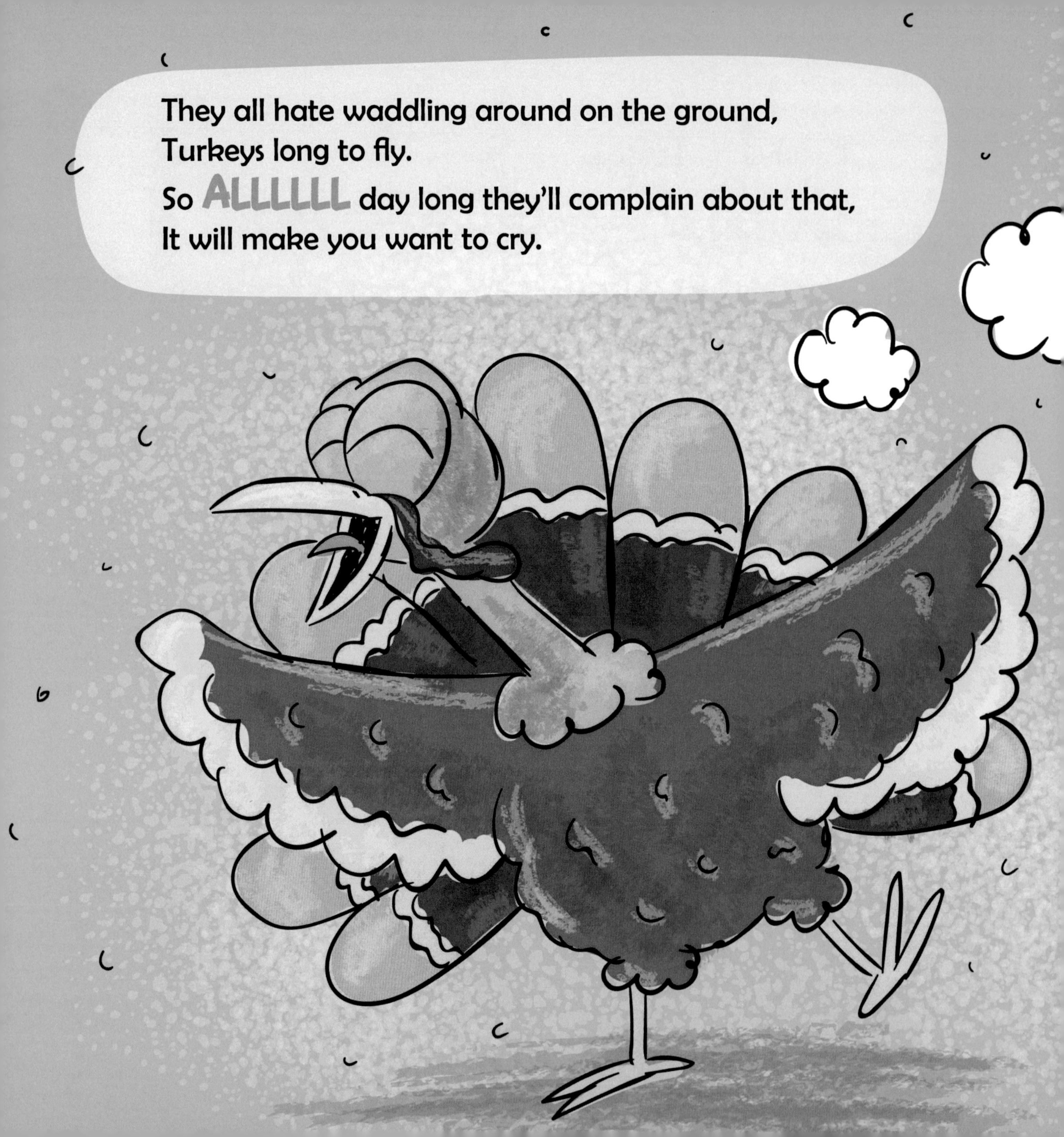

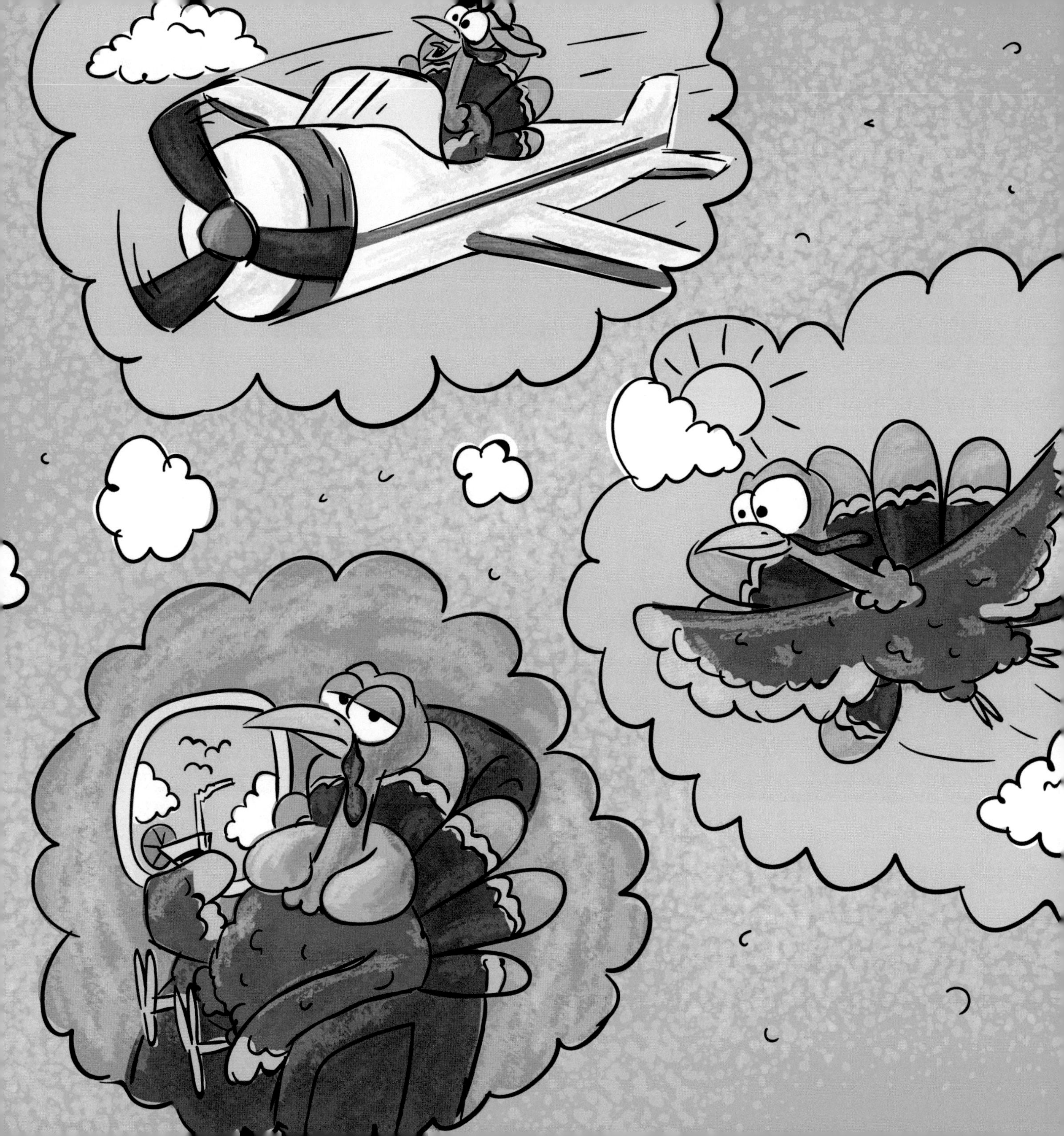

They'll also complain about the meals you serve,
And how they prefer **FANCY** food.
'This dinner tastes like it was cooked by a baby!'
Wow. Turkeys are really quite rude!

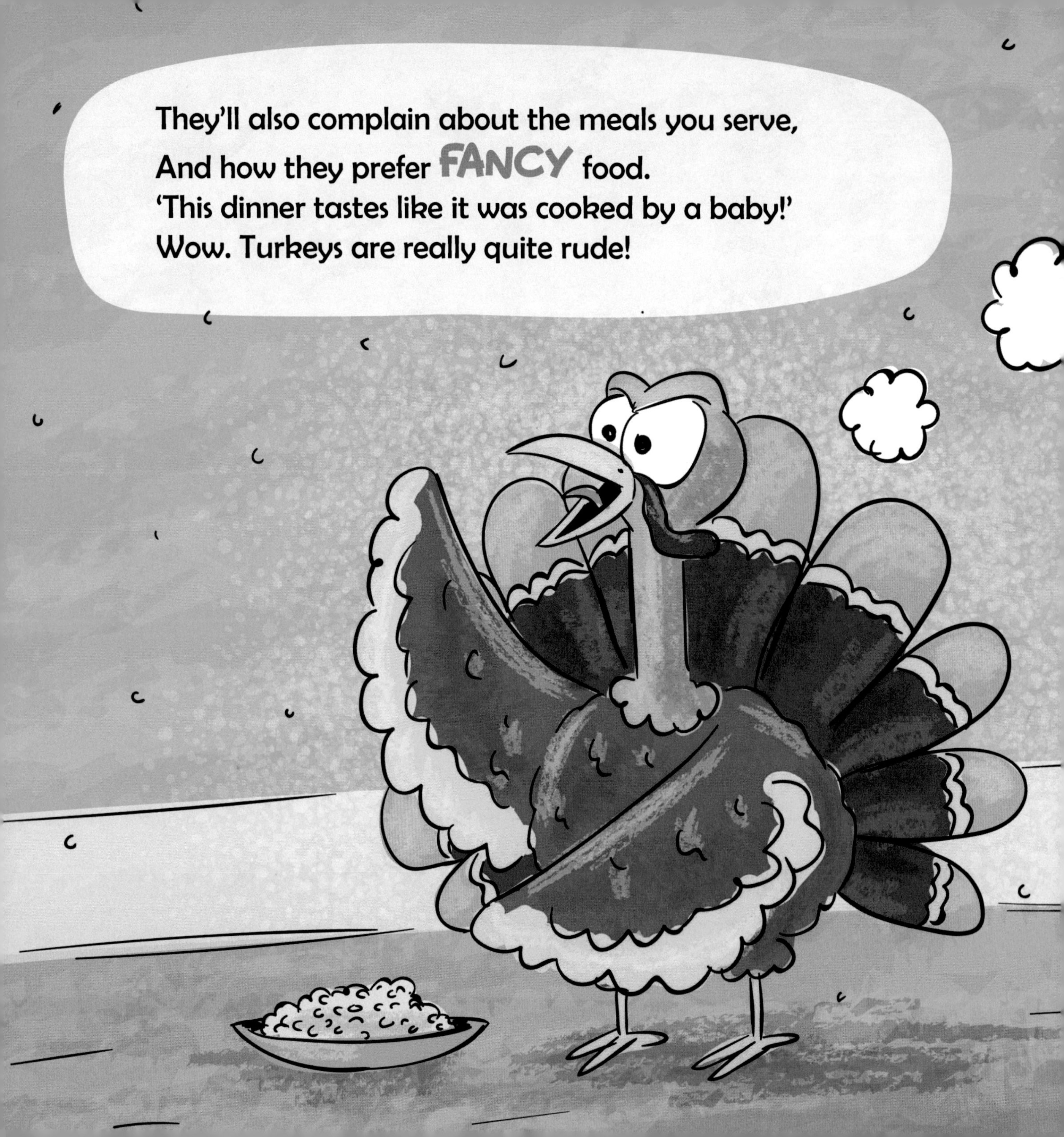

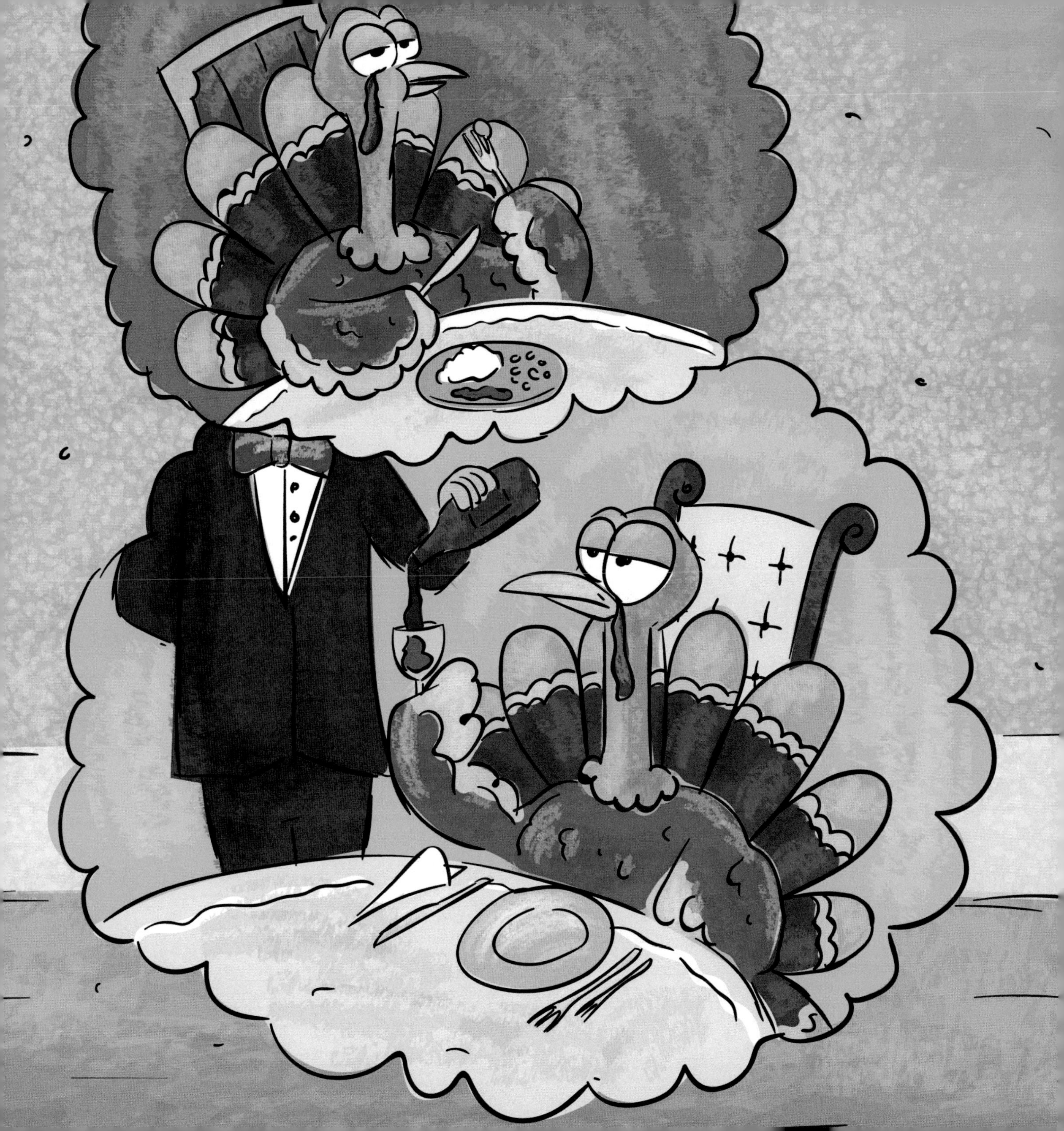

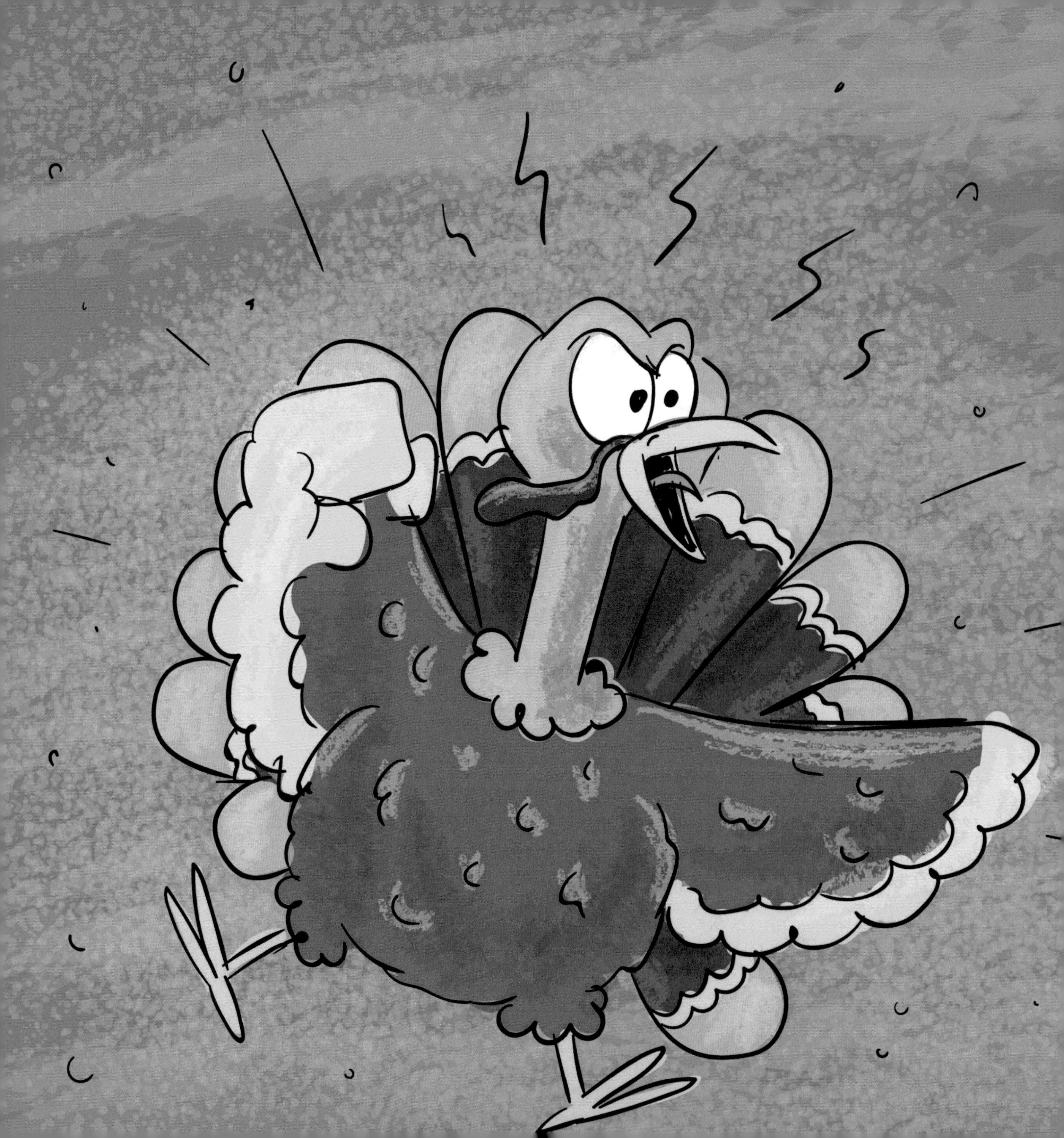

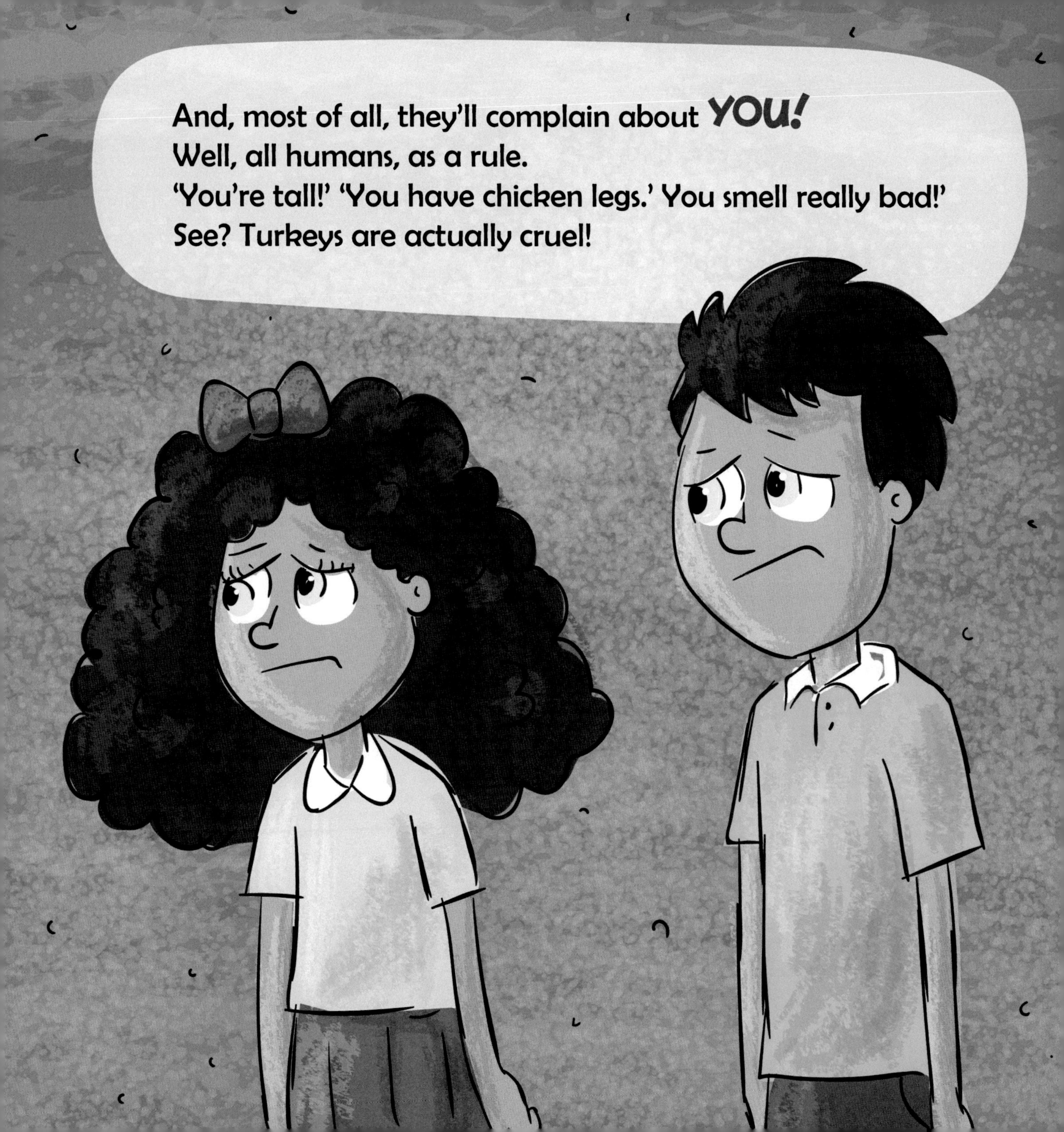
And, most of all, they'll complain about **YOU!**
Well, all humans, as a rule.
'You're tall!' 'You have chicken legs.' You smell really bad!'
See? Turkeys are actually cruel!

So never **EVER** tickle or trust a turkey,
Or translate the words that it said.
If you do, you're only asking for trouble,
So get **THAT** idea out of your head!

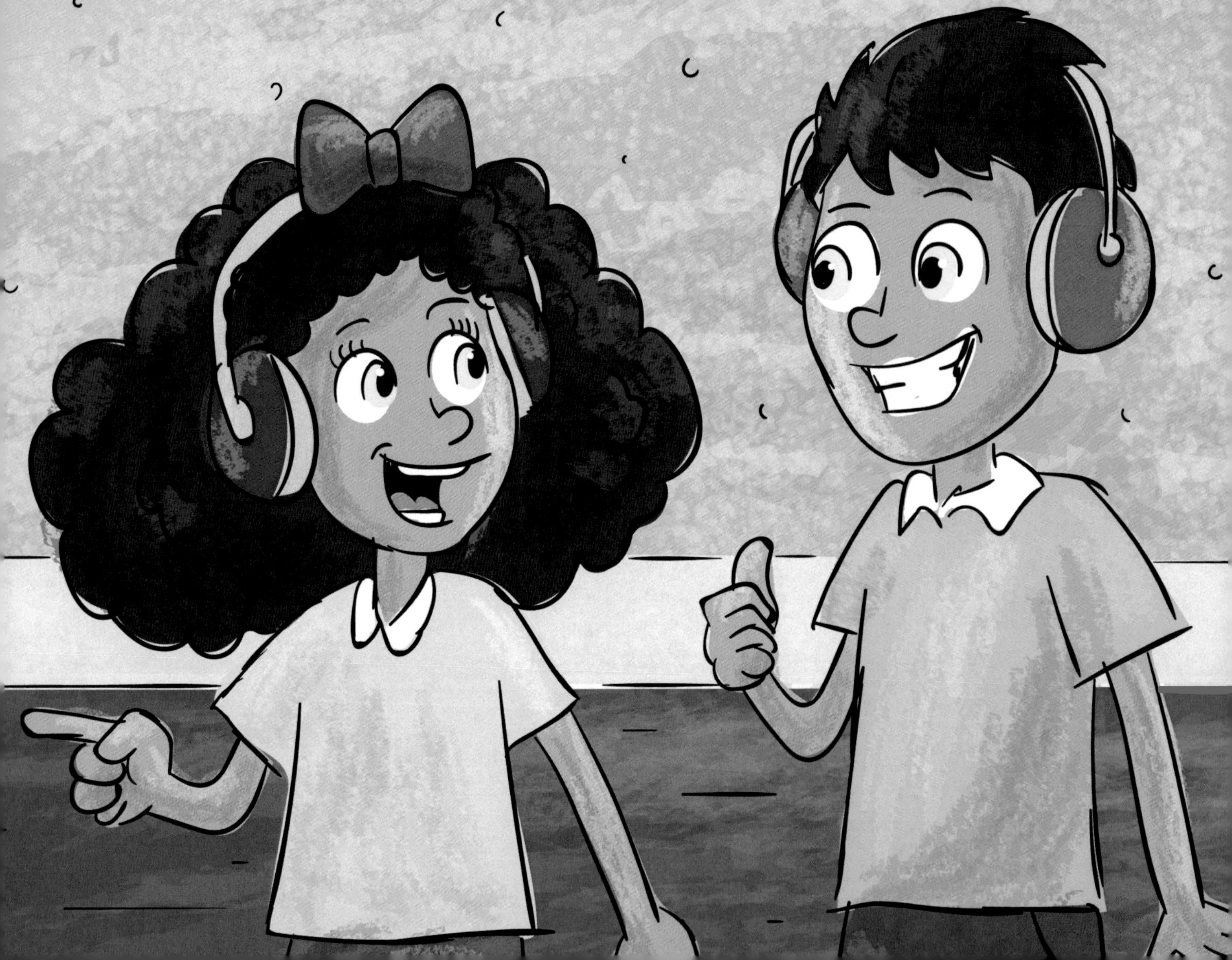

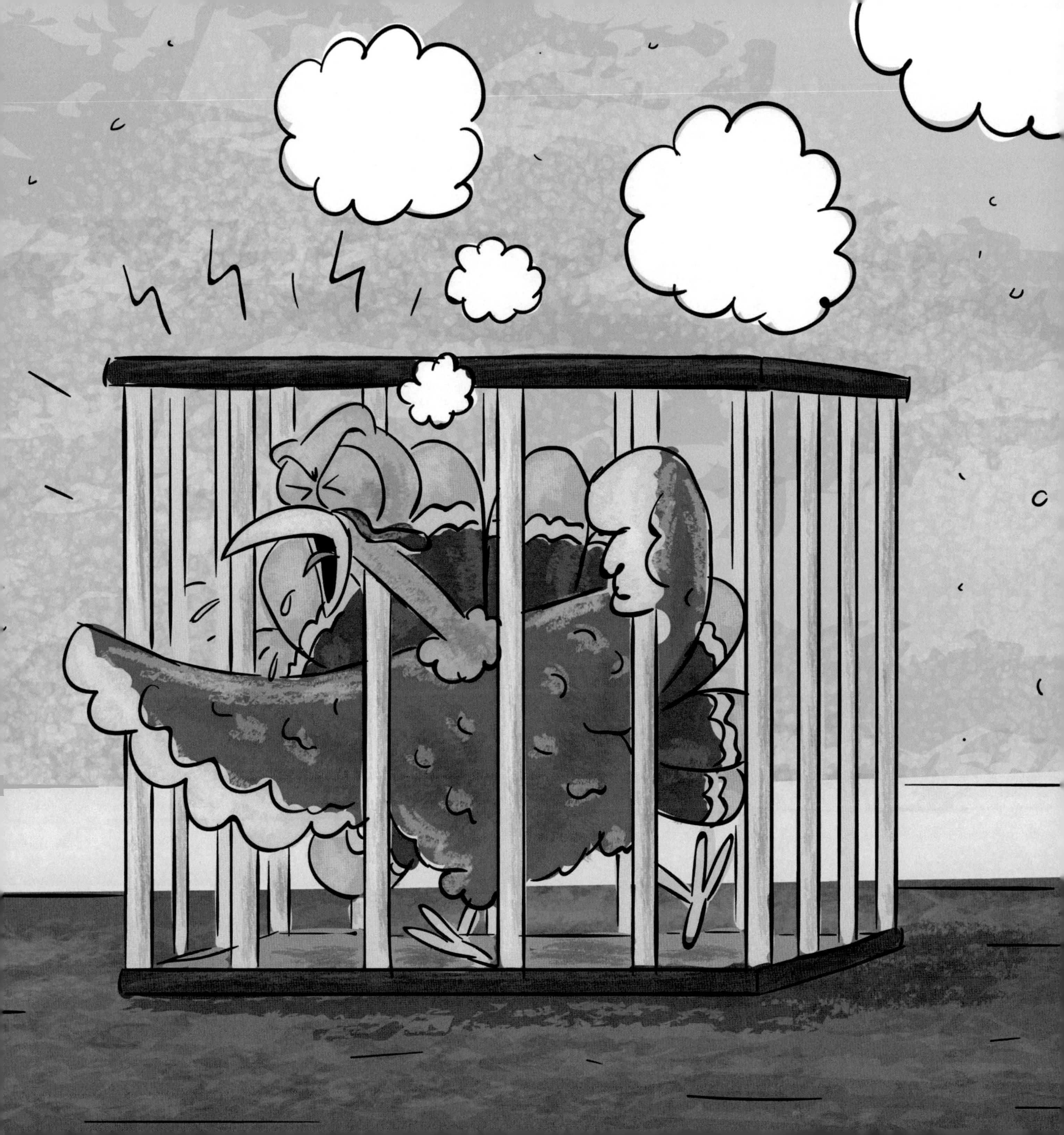

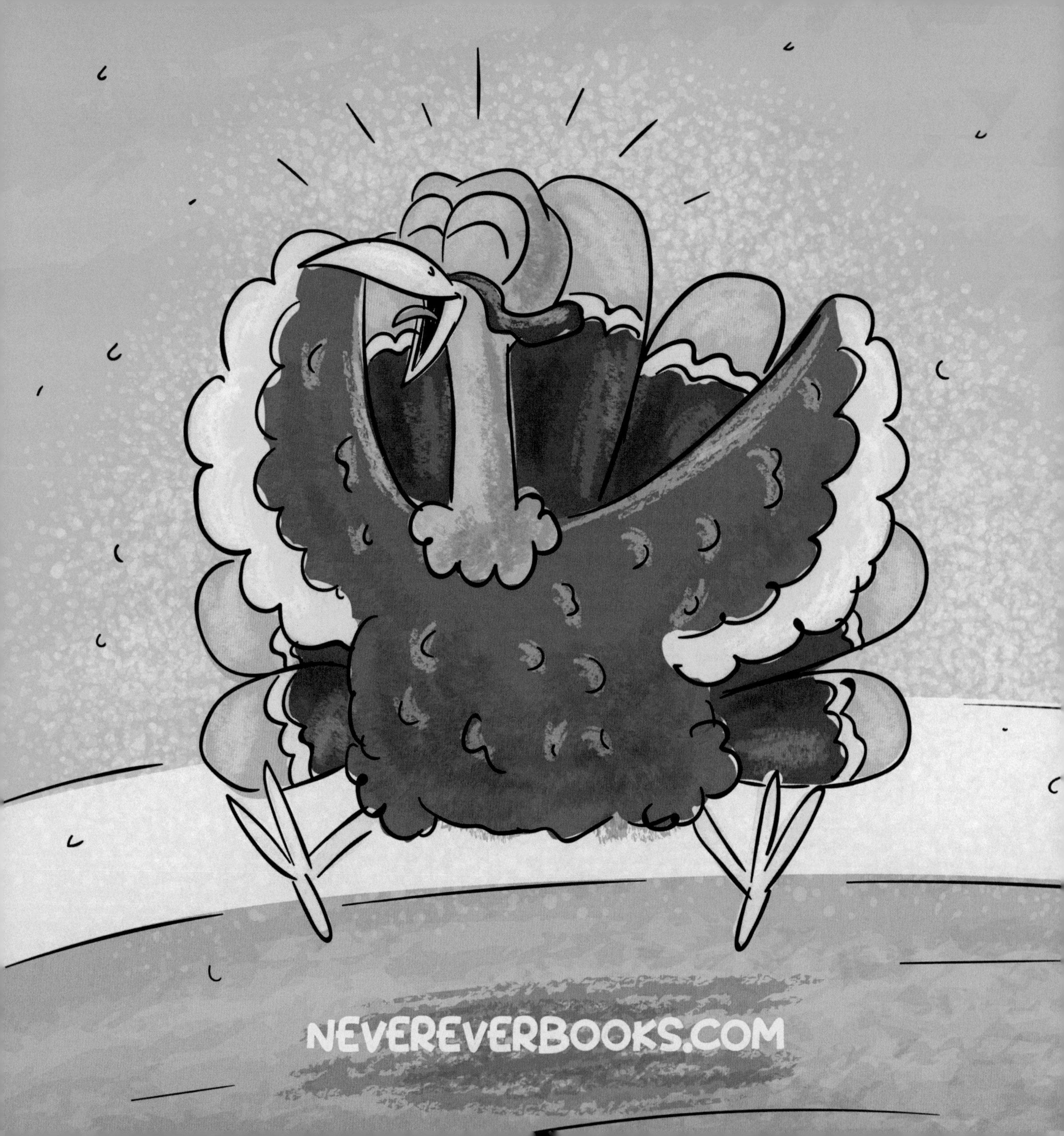
NEVEREVERBOOKS.COM

Mary Nhin Adam Wallace @marynhin

Grow Grit AWallace100 @marynhin

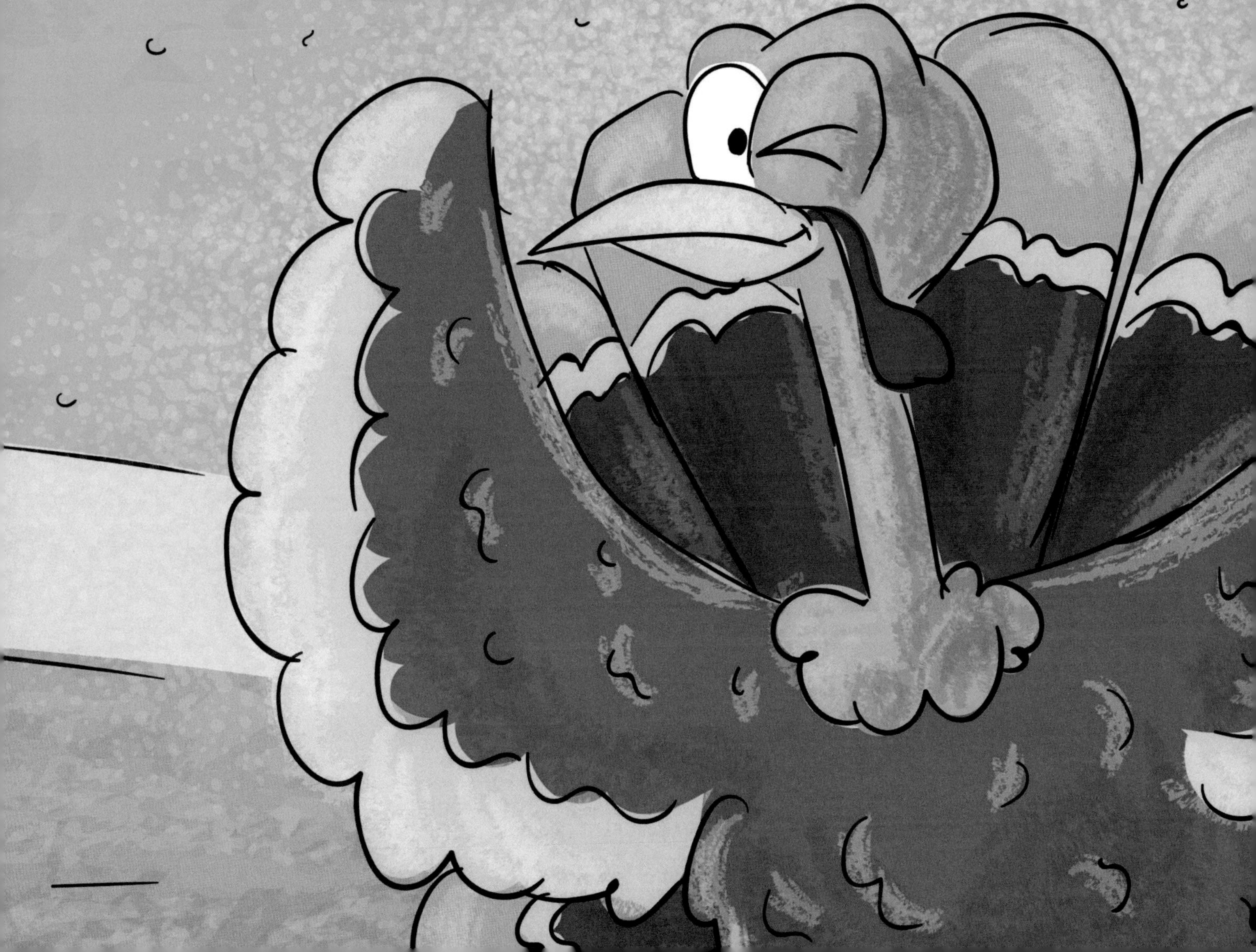

Made in the USA
Monee, IL
03 November 2024

69210471R00021